MARTEK

MARTEK

By
Brian D. Martin

MARTEK

Written & Edited by Brian D. Martin

Front Cover illustrated by Brian D. Martin

Back Cover illustrated by Brian D. Martin
(Revised by Kevin Martin)

All Characters are copyrighted by the creator of this novel, Brian D. Martin. None of these characters have been adopted by existing books or heroes in previous creations by other artists. All characters in this novel were created by Brian D. Martin and are original.

Please be sure to check out the second installment to Martek and his Adventures. Martek II – The Atlas. Coming winter 2008 to your local bookstores!

Thank you for reading!

PROLOGUE
The Very Beginning

Millions of years ago, at a time where life itself was just but a spec of cellular life forms; Earth was just yet a planet out of many. Planets from all around formed from single star systems and were given light to their own binding in which they shared. Each planet's star was indeed a powerhouse to keep life going.

Out of millions of these stars, a planet was formed along side a G-2 yellow star. This planet as we know it today; is Earth. Inside the planetary system revolved a single like rock, which orbited the Earth. This rock as we know it today; is The Moon.

Peering down on the earth we see lush forests, clear air, and many storms brewing along the surface. Volcanoes erupted constantly, and thunderstorms flashed on the dark side of this desolate planet. A single like comet arrived; so bright it out shined the G-2 yellow star. But this was no ordinary comet; for this comet had the most unique components to it unimaginable. Series of energies surrounded the diamond surface of this space rock. Indeed this comet was no ordinary comet; it was a comet made completely out of Diamonds. As the comet hurled through the Solar System, it headed on a collision course toward the neighboring star. The comet smashed into the star with so much force, it created the brightest most massive explosion that could be seen for light years.

Clouds of energies blew toward the outer parts of the solar system; however one large chunk of diamond flew directly into the Earth causing a very large impact.

After the dust from the impact had settled, a tall muscular man lay lifeless inside the crater caused by the impact. The man wore a dark battle suit along with a sword and scabbard. It was apparent that who ever he was, he traveled a great distance.

The man's name is Mathazar, and he is a great sorcerer. He lived on a distant planet much like Earth; only to cause destruction and pain to anyone deems worthy of it. He was the planets most powerful man. Many years ago, Mathazar became so powerful, that no one could step in his way. He obeyed no one but himself, and created many magical feats. Self taught and alone, he grew stronger in power with each waking moment. With no guidelines, he indeed could do anything he wanted. After a while, the people of the planet decided that enough was enough. They got together and attacked Mathazar with everything that they had. After getting a few medicine men to work hard on stopping his power, Mathazar was injected by medicine that would soon later put him into a deep sleep. When he was injected, he fell hard to the ground. Joy sprang throughout the land as celebrations sprung out in every city. This wasn't the end of Mathazar's containment. He was later taken to a lab and closed into liquid diamond, where he was placed in a freezing chamber to be locked away for all eternity. After being completely frozen for days, he was thrown out of the planet and into interstellar space. The only thing that would break his containment is a heat so great; it could melt a diamond.

Stars flickered above his body, which lay face up.

After the time had passed some, twilight started to shine brightly in the sky. It wasn't long until the Star, known as the sun; peeked over the horizon and shone on his body. As the rays of the star hit him, he began to wake up. He moved his head left to right and opened his eyes looking up at the rich blue sky, feeling the warm breeze on his face.

"Where am I?" He said as he slowly got up to look around.

He got up to his feet and found that he was in a crater of dirt. He climbed out and stood there looking down at where he impacted.

"How long has it been? What is this place?" He said while looking around, examining everything in sight. He immediately noticed that the yellow star was not blue. "I can not be home, for this star is yellow." He said thinking.

With powers as strong as his, he flew around the globe to the other side where it was night. There, he noticed that the planet was joined next to a bright circle of light. With a great leap he flew directly out of the Earth and toward the Moon. He found that it was a round space rock that somehow was connected to the Earth. When he looked back at the Earth, a smile came across his face.

"New World, meet Mathazar! I'm home!" His laugh echoed throughout the skies.

When the first week passed by, he noticed new things about his planet. He noticed that the clear liquid was drinkable, and that some fruit was edible. He also noticed that the Moon went around the skies but stayed the same distance signifying a connection between the Moon and his new planet.

As thousands of years passed, he wondered why he had not perished. He saw life born, and life die. The only one that didn't age on this planet was his own self. His immortality was caused by the yellow sun; in which his blue sun aged him greatly. Being under the yellow sun gave him immortal energies. No matter though, every waking century, he only grew stronger and stronger. He trained himself for that one day where he would have a world to defend and take over from anyone who gets in his way.

As the world became more populated, Mathazar was seen by many as a type of God or Guardian. He saw that the Human race was growing and growing; and that he would have to hide in order to stay unseen. After being tired of his immortality, he created a Realm called the Realm of Time. This Realm was his sacred hideout; which no one would ever find. It is a Realm outside of the world and into a created one. The Realm was small, and bright; yet very comforting to him. While inside of the Realm's blue light, he aged every year until he became an old man. After he stepped back out of his Realm, he thought hard on how he would regain power in this now populated world. When he looked up to the sun, it was shadowed by the moon. Suddenly, he had an idea.

Mathazar decided to create two individuals and train them. With a wave of his sword, he threw it into the air and it split into two separate swords. When the sword blades hit the ground he approached the swords and grabbed them by each hand.

"I Mathazar, create you!" He shouted up as he threw the swords into the eclipsed Sun. When the swords hit the eclipsed Sun, two light beams of energy beamed down in front of Mathazar. In an Instant, two very tall, naked, and muscular beings emerged standing before their master. Mathazar walked slowly up to them as a sword appeared in front of each of the two. He went to the one on the right and picked up the sword and walked up to him.

"Kneel." He said.

The being kneeled looking down to the ground as Mathazar placed the sword's blade on top of his head.

"You my Son, will be Solaro; God of the Sun!"

The energy from the Sun shinned yellow onto the blade of the sword and slowly transformed Solaro's body into a fully armored body suit.

Mathazar looked down to his new creation. "Now, stand before me and swear your allegiance to me as your Master."

Solaro stood up. "Yes Master." He bowed.

Mathazar gave him the Sword.

"This sword will give you unbelievable power, use this wisely and never will it fail."

"As you wish Master." Solaro said.

Mathazar looked over to the other being and walked to him and picked up the sword that lay in front of him.

"Kneel." He said.

The being kneeled looking down to the ground as Mathazar placed the sword's blade on top of his head.

"You my Son, will be Lunaro; God of the Moon!"

The energy from the Moon shinned Blue onto the blade of the sword and slowly transformed Lunaro's body into a fully armored body suit as well.

Mathazar looked down to his second new creation.

"Now, you as well must stand before me and swear your allegiance to me as your Master."

Lunaro stood up. "I obey Master." He bowed.

Mathazar gave him the Sword.

"This sword will also give you unbelievable power, use this wisely and never will it fail."

Mathazar backed up and looked at his new creations.

"Okay, now we have much to learn." Mathazar said.

As the years went by, Mathazar trained Solaro and Lunaro in the Realm of Time. The more Solaro learned about Mathazar's plan, the more he yearned for the day. However, the more Lunaro learned; the more he became less interested. Solaro was the evil type, where Lunaro sided more on what was good then what was bad.

Nearing the end of training, Mathazar grew in age and was near the end of his time. Mathazar gathered Lunaro and Solaro and spoke to them one last time.

"Gather around my Sons." He said as he sat down. "As you know, you are training to take control of this planet that I landed on so many years ago. You are to make sure that no one takes that from you. However, the world is now a very dangerous place. You must never destroy this planet until forces cause you to. I created you two because my time grows short. I want you both to carry on my legacy. I trained you as powerful sorcerers, not murderers. Please do not abuse your power. Each sword has a specific power to it; these swords must never come together. If they do, you will destroy this planet and everything in it. You will become consumed in your own power that you will forget who you are hurting. Trust me, I know because it happened to me. This is why I split the power of the swords. Just remember never to let these swords come together. I will be with you always…" His last words as he fell to the ground. His body faded away into the skies. Mathazar was finally dead.

It wasn't long until shortly after his death, one became the leader. Solaro had different intentions and

Lunaro knew about it.

"I know what you are thinking Solaro. Please don't do it." Lunaro said.

"Too late!" Solaro yelled out.

Lunaro held his sword tightly in his hands and knew what he had to do. He jumped out of the Realm and noticed a circle of trees and a fresh green patch of grass behind him. Seconds later, Solaro emerged out of thin air and walked up to him.

"Give me the sword, or die!"

Lunaro knew that he had to fight the greed that flowed inside Solaro.

"Listen to yourself. Our Master told us to never combine these swords. To combine these would mean the end of this world!" Lunaro said backing up.

"Let me deal with that." Solaro said. "Now give me the sword, or die."

Lunaro got into fighting position.

"You want this sword so badly? Come and get it."

Solaro drew his sword and clashed swords with Lunaro. Sparks of energy and light could be seen from the two as they fought to the death.

"I was always the better fighter you know." Solaro said as he sliced Lunaro's arm.

Lunaro held up his hand and his sword as a ball of blue energy formed. He threw it toward Solaro and blasted him onto the ground.

"Oh so if it's a power fight you are asking, then you are going to pay for that!" Solaro said angrily.

Solaro got up quickly and extended his hand toward Lunaro and bolts of electricity flowed out of his finger tips and hit Lunaro onto the forest floor. Just as quick as Lunaro fell, Solaro raced toward him and gave one last stab directly into Lunaro's chest.

"I didn't want it to end this way brother." Solaro

said looking down at Lunaro's bleeding mortal body sitting on his knees.

Lunaro gasped for air in pain, but he knew it was time to die. With one last breath, Lunaro raised his sword. "By the power of the Moon, I cast this sword into the Realm of Power that I create. I shall be resurrected in spirit when one day someone of a pure heart unlocks the Realm. Until then, let no one enter this Realm!" Lunaro threw the sword into the Realm of Power and collapsed on the ground. The sword disappeared from sight, and Lunaro's dead body faded into the air.

"No!" Solaro shouted as he leaped where the sword faded.

Solaro took note on where the sword had disappeared and gathered several stones. He placed the stones in a circle around where he thought the realm was.

"This circle is to remind me where this Realm is. When it is broken, I will return. Until then, I will remain outside of all Realms to ensure that I never age, and also to ensure I destroy anyone who gets in my way.

Solaro laughed out loud in such an evil tone that even the birds flew out of the trees. His laugh echoed throughout the entire land and he faded into the Darkness waiting for the day to come.

CHAPTER 1

On a clear, crisp, but not so cold Spring Morning; there lay a desolate city known as Riverdale. Riverdale was surprisingly without much crime at all. The streets were clear, the litter was not to be seen, and the people were extremely polite. Of course, where there was a city, there was always a crime here and there. Now, Riverdale is not the most perfect place in the world as it does have its ups and downs just like any other city. The city has large tall buildings that tower over most of the suburbs. It's full of businesses and just about everything you can think of in a rather large city. Compared to the City of Los Angeles, Riverdale is about half the size and is located right in a nice desolate valley – with the mountains to the North, the Riverdale Hills to the West, and just beyond that lays a wonderful blue ocean. Sometimes during a nice breeze from the west, the feeling of the cool waters can be felt. To the south lies the Santa Ana River as well as even taller hills; and to the east is a desert that goes on for miles and miles.

Inside of this remarkable looking city lives a teenaged boy named Martek. He is an average teenage boy and is not popular with girls at school. He is mildly thin with tanned skin, Brown eyes, and medium length hair. Standing at only five feet ten inches, he is of course seemingly average. He lives with his mother Sarah in the neighborhood just north of the Santa Ana River and about a mile or so from the Hills of Riverdale. He was born with absolutely no memory of his Father and is an only child.

On a quiet street, the sun was about to come up. Birds started to chirp in the trees that lined the neighborhood. Early morning joggers and kids walked the peaceful streets. Martek's house is a large white one-story home with very green grass out in front.

Inside of the house, down the hall and to the left just before the bathroom is Martek's room.

Riiiinnnggg! Martek's Alarm on his nightstand clock rang into his ear.

He quickly slammed his hand down on top of the clock to shut it off.

"Ugh, Shut up you stupid clock." He said in a frustrated tone.

He took his pillow, flipped over on his stomach, and covered his whole head with the pillow.

"I don't want to get up! I… I Think I'm… Yeah, I am sick; that's it." He laughs.

Then a voice was heard down the hallway.

"Martek…! Martek you better wake up or you're going to be late! Rise and shine young man!"

He heard his Mom and slowly got up.

"Oh great, another day at school."

He quickly got up and out of his bed. He rushed to the bathroom around the corner and shut the door and locked it. He opened up the shower door and reached for the knob to turn it. Once the water was on, he opened the cabinet above the toilet and took out a fresh towel and draped it over the shower door. He quickly undressed and hopped into the shower.

"Ouch, that's a bit too hot for me." He said.

He began to clean up for the day and just as he turned around to rinse his hair, his foot slipped on a piece of soap making him fall to the tile floor.

Sarah was in the kitchen and heard a loud crash down the hall. She grabbed her kitchen towel and wiped her hands and headed to the bathroom door. Sarah was just a few inches shorter than Martek, with long wavy black hair, and dark eyes. She was in her forties but looked like she could be an older sister to Martek.

Martek slowly got up in moderate pain.

Sarah got to the bathroom door and knocked three times.

"Martek, are you okay Hun?" Sarah asked while waiting for an answer.

He heard his Mom and shut off the shower - holding his right arm.

"I'm okay Mom, I just slipped."

"Okay, are you sure?"

"Yes, thanks for asking. I'll be out in a minute."

"Okay dear, I made some pancakes for breakfast."

Martek smiled. "Sounds great Mom, I'll be out in a second."

"Okay, I'll see you at the table." Sarah said and walked back to the kitchen.

He opened the shower door slowly and grabbed for the towel. He dried himself off and went to the mirror above the sink. He brushed the condensation off of the mirror and looked at his right arm. Unable to move his arm normally, he could see that it was badly bruised near his elbow.

"Ouch." He said looking at his arm.

He wrapped the towel around his waist and went back to his room and closed the door. He went to the closet and picked out a thin long sleeved shirt to wear so he can cover his bruise. He picked out a pair of jeans and finished up getting ready. He went to his dresser and took his black baseball cap from the top and placed it backwards on his head.

"There we go; all ready now." He said.

On his way to the door he grabbed his backpack and headed for the dining room table.

He walked down the hall and into the dining room table where a plate of pancakes and other good foods were waiting for him.

"Mmmm." Martek said while he got ready to sit down.

"Hey, did you sleep well?" Sarah said.

"I did. How did you sleep?"

"Oh I slept okay. Are you okay? You seem like something is bothering you."

Unable to keep his focus off of the pain in his right arm, he knew that his Mom was starting to catch on.

"I'm okay."

"Well, let me sit down with you and have breakfast, and you can tell me all about it."

"No, its okay, I am fine... Really, I am." Martek said holding his arm.

"Okay, I just thought that you'd be happy today. What's wrong with your arm?"

Martek rolled up his sleeve and showed his mom the bruise that he had on his arm.

"Ouch, are you okay? How did that happen?"

"I'm fine mom; I slipped in the shower."

"Okay Hun."

"So what about that part when you said I'd be happy about today? What exactly is today?"

"Martek, you've been going on about it for days. Its Friday today and tomorrow is your birthday. Surely now you didn't forget your own birthday."

Sarah laughed.

Martek had gone through so much this morning already that he forgot his own birthday.

"Yeah... Of course I remembered Mom. What kind of guy do you think I am?" He laughed along.

"Okay good, cause you still have not told me what you wanted for your birthday."

"Well Mom, how about a birthday party? I know I have asked you but I am turning seventeen and this will be my last birthday as an actual teenager. Please?"

"Well, I am sure it would be okay, but on such short notice?"

"I know, I'll only invite my friends that I hangout with at lunch. You know I don't have many friends Mom."

"Oh Martek, don't you say that. You have many friends."

"Well, I am guessing around ten or so people. Is that okay?"

"That is fine." Sarah agreed

"What time should the party start?" Martek asked.

"Well let's do this. How about the party will start at 10am and end at around 6pm?"

"Okay that sounds perfect."

"Alright, then we'll order pizzas for lunch."

"Wow that sounds great Mom!"

"How are you going to get invitations to your friends?" Sarah asked.

"I'll write them up and give the invitations to them. If I don't see them I'll find a way to get them the message."

"Okay, I was just wondering because this is at

short notice." She smiled.

They sat there and finished up with breakfast.

Several minutes later Martek got up from the table and pushed in his chair.

"Great breakfast Mom." He said while putting his plate in the kitchen sink.

"Thank you Hun. Are you ready for school?"

"Yeah, I'm all ready. Are you ready for work?" He smiled.

"Yes, I just have to grab my briefcase and we'll leave."

Sarah was a morning News Anchorwoman for the KCRT Channel Seven News Network every weekday morning at seven. She had a great stable job, and it worked perfectly around her everyday schedule.

Sarah got up and cleaned up the kitchen table quickly and headed for her room. She grabbed her briefcase and made sure she had everything, including her car keys and headed for the door.

"All ready Martek?" She said while turning off all of the house lights except for the porch light.

"Yup, I got everything, let's get going so we aren't late."

"You're late? It's twenty after six and you think you are late." She laughed.

Martek and Sarah opened the garage door and walked into the garage. Sarah shut the door behind her and locked it.

"You got your house key?" She asked.

"Yes, I have it right here." Martek said pulling out the house key from inside of his pocket.

"Okay, I was just making sure just in case you needed it."

Sarah pressed her car alarm button and the car doors unlocked. Both of them got in. The car was a brand new Silver 2001 Honda Accord LX. It had four doors and pretty much everything you could think of, with the exception of any GPS tracking and Road Maps built in. Over all, it was simple and a great vehicle. Martek sat down in the passenger seat and reached behind him to grab the seat belt, and pulled it over to click it in place. He placed his backpack on his knees. Sarah turned on the ignition, and the car ran as silent as a mouse. A sound could barely be heard from the engine. She reached up to the overhead mirror and pressed the garage door button, and the garage door started to open. When the door opened she shifted the vehicle in reverse and backed down the driveway.

"Hey Mom when I get my license; you are going to let me drive this car. Aren't you?" He put a large grin on his face.

"Maybe; just as long, as you don't turn this car into the latest Christmas tree ornament design." She said giving him back a rather large grin.

"Oh Mom, you know I am not *that* bad!" He laughed.

"Yeah I know." She said as she shifted into drive and headed down the street.

"It's a good thing that my bus stop is only two blocks from here isn't it."

"Yeah, well if I had it my way, I would make you walk to the bus stop, but we are both off to a late start so I'll take you today."

"Deal." Martek said.

Just as they rounded the corner, they saw that the bus was parked at the bus stop with the kids already inside.

"Oh great, the bus is going to leave." Martek said.

"Not if I have anything to do with it, it'll stay right where it is until you are on that bus."

Martek looked over at his Mom and nodded his

head smiling.

The bus doors closed and just as the bus driver was pulling out, Sarah pulled right in front of the bus, which forced the bus to come to a complete stop.

"Thanks Mom." Martek said giving his Mom a kiss on the cheek.

"Have a good day now. I'll see you after school."

Martek rushed out of the car and ran to the bus. Sarah drove off and the bus driver opened the bus doors for Martek. He rushed up the stairs.

"Now bus driver, either I'm really late or you are really early." Martek said as he walked up the steps.

"You're late. Have a seat Martek." The bus driver said smiling.

Martek headed to the middle of the bus and found his friends John, Druid, and Eric sitting down. John was a little shorter than Martek. He had black hair and dark brown eyes. John was Spanish but his Father was Italian. Druid was taller than Martek, standing at six feet tall. He spent a lot of his spare time in the gym and he was one of the biggest guys at the school. He had brown spiked hair and brown eyes. Eric was an African American boy with both parents being officers of the Riverdale Police. He had buzzed black hair and stood just as tall as Martek. Martek took a seat next to them right across from Eric and in back of Druid and John. The bus pulled onto the street.

"Hey guys, what's up?" Martek asked.

"Not too much man; wow it's your birthday tomorrow. So, what are you going to do?" Druid said.

"Actually, that is what I wanted to ask you guys. I am having a birthday party tomorrow and I wanted to know if you guys wanted to come over?"

"Hey count me in." John said.

"Yeah me too, you know I'm in." Druid said.

"Count me in too, Martek. I am sure that my

parents won't mind." Eric added.

"Alright guys, that sounds great. The party is tomorrow at ten o'clock sharp."

"Ten in the morning?" Asked Eric.

"No you goof, ten at night." Druid said.

Everyone laughed

While everyone was busy having their own fun on the bus, Martek stared with a blank mind out of the window. With his eyes, he followed a few birds flying right next to the bus through the trees. The bus crossed the Santa Ana River Bridge and the birds flew across the river gliding close to the water. One of the birds took a drink, and they all flew straight up over the bus, and out of sight. Martek thought it would be cool to be that free, yet nearly impossible to do most of those things.

Just past the river and onto the left, they came to the street where the high school was located. The street was called Riverdale Drive.

Druid tapped Martek's shoulder. "Hey, Martek, are you okay?" He asked.

They all laughed as Martek jumped up as if he had seen a ghost.

"Ha Ha, you were spacing out there Martek. What's up?" Eric said laughing.

"Nothing, I was just thinking that's all." Martek replied.

"Hey Martek, "Druid said." Did you do the English Homework for Mrs. Maine's class?"

"Oh no, I forgot!"

"That's okay, you're in my class that period and remember we are going to be watching a movie today in class, but the homework was supposed to be done and turned in today."

"Yeah, I totally forgot. I have PE in first period, then English with you in second."

"Yeah, I have an idea. Why don't you take this

paper and copy all the answers off during P.E. and you can give it back to me before class starts. Just do not, copy word for word; make your own sentence but make sure the answer is good enough."

"Really Druid? I can do that?"

"Of course you can. Hey I remember when I was stuck in a situation like this and you saved my hide so take this paper."

"Wow, thanks man, you are a life saver." Martek said taking the paper and putting it inside his notebook."

Eric cut in. "Just one thing Martek."

"What's that?"

"Well, Mrs. Wells hates it when you skip P.E. How are you going to skip it?"

Martek rolled up his right sleeve, which exposed his right arm up to his elbow.

"Ouch! Dude that bruise is sick!" Eric said.

"Yeah man. How did you get that? John asked.

"I got it this morning. I accidentally slipped in the shower, and ate it pretty bad on the tile."

"That looks like it hurts, and I know for sure that Mrs. Wells is going to excuse you today." Eric added.

Martek smiled. "Exactly."

Moments later the bus arrived at the Riverdale High School.

The bus pulled into the bus zone and came to a stop. Like always, all of the students got up and rushed to the exit right before the bus driver even opened up the doors. Martek and Eric got up, but Druid was already pushing his way through the line that led to the front of the bus. Druid was of course the biggest guy on the bus, so nobody said anything and they just let him pass by. John used Druid as a shield and followed his path to get out of the bus faster. Martek and Eric didn't really care. They knew that everyone would eventually get off of the bus so they didn't worry.

Martek and Eric finally got off of the bus and Druid and John were standing just outside of it laughing.

"What's so funny Druid?" Martek asked.

Martek and Eric walked up to John and Druid.

"Oh nothing Martek. Just that… you and Eric are slow pokes!" They laughed.

"Ha ha, very funny." Eric said.

They all laughed.

Druid looked at his watch and told them that they had about a few minutes until the bell rang.

Martek decided to leave to class. "Hey guys, since we have a few minutes, I'm going to start walking to class. I'll see you in second period Druid. Later guys." Martek said.

"Bye Martek." They all said.

"Martek wait. I'll go with you since we have the same class." Eric said rushing to Martek.

Martek and Eric started to walk to class.

"So, what are you going to say to Mrs. Wells?"

"That's easy man, the truth. I'll tell her that I hit my arm and I'll even show it to her; she will have to excuse me from class. The pain isn't as bad as it was before, but it still hurts quite a bit."

"Alright man, that's cool. I am not really looking forward to P.E. either."

"Why is that?"

"Well… You know why."

"Oh not again, you need to learn to stand up for yourself Eric. In fact, you need to just ignore everything altogether that bugs you."

"I know I do, but he still has a problem because of his Father."

"It's not your fault his Father turned out to be a jailbird."

"Yeah I know. I guess this is what I get for being the son of two cops."

They both laughed.

The bell rang to go to first period and everyone started to head for class. The sun was shinning bright, and the weather was increasingly warmer than usual, but nobody minded because it was a nice morning. Martek and Eric went into the Men's Locker room and went to change into their P.E. gear. Eric's locker was right across from Martek's in the same isle. Martek entered his combination and unlocked his lock to open the locker. He put some books into his locker and closed it. After locking up, Eric was just about ready. The High School Football players had their lockers across from the showers on the other side of the locker room.

Martek turned to Eric who was tying his shoe.

"Are you ready yet?"

"Just about, let me get this last shoe… Got it, lets go."

Martek and Eric walked out of the locker room and onto the blacktop. The blacktop had a place for each class. Each class consisted of a square of numbers, which each student was assigned a specific number. Mrs. Wells' class was right behind both locker rooms. Martek was number ten, Eric being number six.

All of the kids were running right as the tardy bell rang. Most of the class was already standing on their numbers, but Martek was the only one not dressed, and with his backpack on. People were looking at him and wondered why he wasn't in his P.E. clothes.

"Hey Martek!" One of the students said from another class. "Why aren't you dressed?"

"Hey Brian, I am not doing anything today. I am being excused."

"Oh ok. I'll talk to you later man." Brian replied.

"You got it!" Martek said.

Martek and Eric got to their numbers and stood on them.

Just then a football came close to hitting Eric in the head. Both of them turned to see the football players practicing out on the field behind their class right next to the tennis courts.

"Missed him!" One of the players said.

Martek walked over to the football and tossed it to one of the players, who were running to get it. The player caught the ball and ran back.

"Chicken!" A voice said from the crowd of players.

Eric looked over and it was Rodney Burns, the Senior Quarterback for the Riverdale High Jaguars.

Rod was the biggest guy in school, just a bit bigger than Druid. No one messed with him. He looked like he was on something, but he wasn't. He stood over six feet tall and out weighed Martek and Eric put together.

"What are you looking at you shrimp?" Rod said angrily to Eric. "Want me to come over there and put this football up your..."

"That's enough Rod, get back in the game!" The coach yelled.

"Coming Coach. I'll see you at lunch shrimp boy." He laughed as he joined the rest of the team.

"Don't worry about it man, Rod is trying to upset you."

"Well he is doing a pretty good job at it." Eric said, now angry as all can get.

Martek looked at the number under his feet

"Ha ha. I'm a perfect ten." Martek said to Eric jokingly.

"Bite me." He laughed. "Wonder where Mrs. Wells is at?"

"Who cares?"

Both laughed.

Then the sound of a loud whistle rang into the

morning air.

"Spoke too soon." Eric said.

Mrs. Wells walked onto the blacktop wearing her sunglasses, and holding her blue folder. The blue folder contained all of her student's grades and information; it was her "Bible" some called it. She approached the front of her class. Everyone was standing on their numbers and facing forward. She was a scary old looking woman with short curly white hair, and in her early fifties. She always wore those sunglasses, even in the rain. Everyone thought it was pretty crazy.

"Alright everyone; good morning."

"Good Morning Mrs. Wells." The class said.

"Alright, I will be calling out your names. When you hear your name, let me know if you are here, or you will get an F for the day."

She began to read out all of the names and got to Martek's.

"Martek."

"Here."

"Martek. Why aren't you dressed for PE?" She asked.

"Well Mrs. Wells, my arm isn't feeling too good."

"Did you bring a doctor's note?"

"No I didn't."

"Then I can't excuse you."

Martek pulled up his sleeve and looked at her.

"Now you can." He said in a soft tone.

Gasps from the class were heard from those who could see Martek's entire elbow bruised up badly.

"Oh, wow Martek that looks pretty bad." Mrs. Wells said. "Did you go to the doctor?"

"I just got it this morning when I woke up."

"Have you seen the school nurse?"

"No I am fine. It hurts a bit, but if I could sit out today, that'd be great."

"Yes, you can sit out today, and then take the weekend to recover."

Martek smiled. "Thanks Mrs. Wells."

"Yeah."

Mrs. Wells excused Martek and put an A for the day next to his name.

After role call, she began to talk about today's activities.

"Alright class, today we are going to start a new sport, which is Tennis."

The class was excited because it was a nice clean sport, and rather fun to play.

"You will be assigned four people per team. If you do not know how to play, I will teach you. For those of you who are not playing; when I dismiss you to the tennis court, you will sit on the bench outside of the tennis court."

When Mrs. Wells read off the groups, it was clear that Eric and Martek were not in the same group. This made Martek and Eric a bit upset but they couldn't do anything about it. The class was dismissed to the tennis courts, and everyone walked to the courts.

Martek took a seat next to the tennis courts on the bench. He set his backpack down and unzipped it to take out his folder. He got his folder and opened it to take out Druid's paper and copy down the homework. He knew it was cheating, but he just needed to get something so he can turn in the homework and not receive any detention. He began to do his homework.

Right before the class bell rang; Martek finished up his homework and put it in his folder. He put the folder back in his backpack and closed it up.

The bell rang and Martek grabbed his backpack and put it on. Eric ran toward Martek.

"Hey Martek, wait up!" Eric yelled.

Martek waited for Eric.

Both of them went back into the locker room to get ready for second period. When they were getting ready, the football players came running in acting all tough, banging all the walls with their helmets and what ever they could use. They rushed through the locker isle like a fierce tidal wave going ashore, wiping out other students in their path.

"Don't worry man, forget about everything." Martek said while looking at Eric.

He noticed that Eric was watching his back an awful lot more than on other days. Eric was indeed terrified of Rod Burns; that was a given. Eric finished up getting into his school clothes.

"Yeah, I know... Come on, let's go. Are you ready to go?" Eric said.

"Yeah, let's go."

Martek and Eric locked up their lockers, and headed out of the locker room to join the line of students waiting to be dismissed.

"So did you get done with the homework from Druid?"

"Oh yeah, I'm glad that everything worked out good."

"Me too, you wouldn't want after school detention the day before your birthday." Eric laughed.

"No, of course not." Martek laughed along.

Riiiinnng!!

"Well, that's the bell. I'll see you at lunch." Eric said.

"You bet man. And don't worry about lunch okay. I am sure things will be fine. You just need to learn to stand up for yourself that's all."

"Yeah... Maybe."

Eric walked to his class, and Martek went to the right and around the "A" Building. He went through the door and down the hall and saw Druid just outside of the classroom wearing sunglasses.

"Druid, what's up?"

"Nothing much, you got the goods homie?"

"Yeah man, I got it right here."

Martek pulled Druid's homework out of his backpack and handed it to him. Druid took the paper looking from left to right and folded it up, and slipped it into his pocket.

"Man… What in the world are you doing?" Martek started to laugh.

"I'm just messing with you..."

"Well if that wasn't obvious to anyone, I don't know what is. That looked like we were selling drugs on campus or something."

Both of them laughed hysterically.

"Yeah well, you know me. Let's get our butts in class before Mrs. Maines has ours." Druid said.

Martek and Druid rushed into class and sat down just on time. Seconds later the bell rang and Mrs. Maines got up from her desk to address the class.

"Morning everybody; today we will be watching a film about our lessons we have been learning for the past couple months. After this we will be learning about the Anglo Saxons and their history."

"Awe..." The entire class said in depression and boredom.

"Now class, let's not be hasty. This will be one of the best subjects you will learn in this class. Now, I'd like for you all to take out your homework, and pass it up to the person at the front of the class. Keep passing up your papers until the person in the front row of each row has all of the papers."

The class began to get out their homework and passed it up to the front. As the papers were being brought up, one of the students raised his hand.

"Mrs. Maines." He said.

"What is it Jeffery?"

"I… Well… My dog *really* ate my homework."

The whole class busted up laughing. Some of the students thought it was so funny, they fell to the floor and just broke into tears of joy.

"Class, settle down right now!" Mrs. Maines shouted. "Jeffery that isn't funny at all nor is this an acceptable excuse. What are you doing after school?"

"Well Mrs. Maines… I was thinking about going to hangout with some friends, maybe."

"Well you can cancel that little plan of yours. I warned the entire class about not turning in their homework. When the movie starts, come to my desk to receive a detention."

"Okay." Jeffery said with a blank look on his face.

Glad Druid let me use his homework. Martek thought.

"Alright class, lately we have been learning about the middle ages, but our prime era is during the time where the Knights of the Round Table lived. Can anyone tell me what these years were called?"

Martek raised his hand.

"Martek." Mrs. Maines said as she pointed at him.

"The Knights of the Round Table lived in the Arthurian Years, which the legendary King Arthur ruled."

"Very good Martek; can anyone tell me who King Arthur's teacher was?"

Martek raised his hand quickly, and then a few other hands rose.

"Jimmy, can you tell me?"

"Yes I can. When King Arthur was growing up, he was taught by a powerful Wizard. The Wizard's name was Merlin."

"Very good Jimmy and one more important

question… What was the name of the sword that made Arthur the most historical King on record?"

Druid raised his hand first.

"Druid, do you know the answer?"

"The answer is Excalibur. I remember this one hotel that I stayed at in Las Vegas. Other than that, I might not really know but thank God for that hotel resort."

The class laughed.

"Very interesting, Druid. I'd hoped you remember it by what you are supposed to be *learning* in class, rather then all of your trips to Las Vegas."

Druid smiled not knowing what else to say.

Mrs. Maines put the tape inside of the VHS player and the movie started. All of the students watched with surprisingly barely any talking at all. At one part of the movie, Martek saw Arthur pulling Excalibur from the stone. He was intrigued that one sword was able to give one man so much power. He turned over to Druid who was sitting right next to him.

"This is my favorite part." Martek said.

"Yeah, this is a pretty neat part."

"Watch how he easily gets the sword in his hands, and yet it took thousands before him who failed. It's a classic!"

"Yeah, it's amazing how the legend has things that will never happen in this lifetime. Kind of makes you think. Doesn't it?"

"Yeah, that is true."

Martek stared back at the movie with blank opened eyes. A dark vale covered his thoughts and Martek was put into a deep day dream. Minutes later, the movie was over and the bell for lunch echoed through campus.

CHAPTER 2

Martek and Druid walked toward the area where they hung out at lunch. The skies were clear blue, and not a cloud was visible in the sky. The air was warm; as a typical spring afternoon should be. When they both got to the lunch line, they parted ways.

"Alright man, I'll see you in a bit." Druid said.

"Alright, I'll catch you later."

Druid headed toward the group they all hung out with at lunch.

"Hey." Eric said walking up to Martek.

Martek was waiting in the lunch line for Eric and he caught up with him.

"Hey Eric, what's up?"

"Not too much, just enjoying a nice warm day."

"Yeah, it is a nice day isn't it?"

"So what are you going to get for lunch today?" Eric asked.

"Honestly, everything on the menu looks great, but I think I'll go with the sub sandwich, chips, and a sugar cookie."

"Yum, that sounds good. Today, I guess I'll have the pizza. After all, it is pizza Friday!"

"Awesome choice man, just let the campus lunch lady know." He smiled.

When Martek got to the end of the line, he started to order up what he wanted for lunch.

"Alright, I want a Roast Beef Sub Sandwich. Then I'll have those Barbequed Chips, and that sugar cookie."

"Okay, anything else you'd like?" The lunch lady asked.

"No. That'd be about it."

"Okay, your total is two-fifty."

Martek reached into his pocket and pulled out a small wad of dollar bills. He took out three of the bills and handed them to the lunch lady. The lunch lady put the money inside of the register, and gave him back two quarters.

"Thank you." Martek said taking the quarters.

When both of them had their lunches, they left to the group of friends that they hung out with every lunch. The group was located right next to the ASB building on the steps that lead up to the ASB windows. Usually those windows on the building were closed, so you would have to end up getting into the building by the side door just right of the building. They walked through the outdoor hall and toward the P.E. locker rooms. The ASB building was located left of the gym, right next to the men's locker room. When they got there, they could see all of their friends including John and Druid. Druid was talking everyone's ear off with his many jokes that he liked to say during lunch. Everyone did like that as they laughed each time he finished the joke. John saw Martek and Eric walking up to the group.

"Hey Martek. Hey Eric. Glad you two could make it. What took so long?" John yelled out.

Martek and Eric walked closer and closer.

"What's up John? Martek said. "You know, the lines get longer and longer each year. I remember in freshman year the lines weren't half as bad, but so many people are moving into this city they might have to build another school." Martek said as he got closer to the group.

When they got to the group, they both started to eat their lunch. Druid saw that Martek and Eric were at the group. He finished up his joke and headed to talk to both of them and John, who was in on the conversation.

"Hey guys, what's up?" Druid said walking up to them.

"Not much man, just eating lunch and hanging out a bit." Eric said.

"Cool, cool. What about you Martek?" Druid asked.

"Same, just eating. Thanks again for the homework; that was a relief."

"Hey, no problem man; anytime."

"Same here." Martek smiled.

Druid turned to Eric.

"So buddy, what is this I hear about you and Rod at P.E. today?"

"Look, it wasn't me who started it; it was him. I was minding my own business like always, and he and his stupid friends had to pick on me, and I really hate that. Sometimes I think it's because I am not White or something."

"Now Eric, it was your parents. Color has nothing to do with it my friend." Martek jumped in and said.

"Yeah, I know Martek, that's easy for you to say."

"Easy for me to say? It should be way easier for Druid to say because he is twice my size."

"Well just because I am twice your size bro doesn't mean anything." Druid added. "Size doesn't matter when people fight. The lighter weight people can move way faster most of the time. The only advantage a guy my size would have is his strength and power behind a nice good solid punch. Guys like you and Eric would easily be able to hit one after one, and keep doing it that way until the fight is over."

"Okay Druid, now that's way easy for you to say. I can't take Rod on." Eric said.

"Look Eric, just because you can't win in a fight doesn't mean anything." Martek said. "It is okay to lose a fight, and the best part of it is that you tried. It only matters if you tried and nothing else. But seriously dude, you have to learn to stand up for yourself including to people like Rod. If you don't get your head out of your rear, you'll be picked on for life." Martek said.

"Just stand up for yourself man." John added in.

Eric was looking down to the ground in heavy thought. He knew that he needed to stand up to Rod one day, but he didn't want it to be so soon.

Just then, Druid looked up to see a few people walking toward them. Martek caught on and looked behind him to see who it was.

"Oh great, not now." Martek said shaking his head.

Eric looked and saw Rod and his two buddies on his side walking up to the group.

"Oh no, what do I do?" Eric asked in fright.

"Don't worry man; just keep your guard up." Druid said to Eric.

"My guard up... What guard? I have no guard! Why can't you fight him for me?"

"Easy," Druid said. "One, this is not my fight.

And two, I am not a fighter. I may workout in the gym a lot, but I'll never fight for any reason. Yeah, if he wanted to fight me then okay I'd do it."

Rod pushed his way through the crowd until he got to Eric. Martek was standing just to the right of Eric and Druid was a bit on the left and toward the wall behind them. Everyone else backed away from Rod extremely quick as they knew Rod wasn't at all in a good mood.

Rod walked up the stairs with his two buddies to his left and his right. Eric didn't make a move as he was frozen in fear; Martek on the other hand was the closest to Eric and was not going to move away.

"Well look who it is. I told you I was going to see you at lunch you little twerp." Rod said.

Rod walked up the stairs until he was face to face with Eric. Eric was a lot shorter than Rod so all he could do was look up to his face and not breathe.

Pretty soon a small crowd of people gathered around Rod and Eric, which was getting larger and larger by the second. All of the students knew that there was going to be a fight and when Rod was involved, they knew it would be a good one.

"Uh… What do you want Rod?" Eric said stuttering.

"What do you mean what do I want? You don't ask me what I want, you know what I want pal."

"Why can't you just leave me alone, Rod?"

"Leave you alone?" Rod chuckled. "Why should I… Leave you alone?"

"Look, it isn't my fault about your Dad and my parents. Your Dad broke the damn law and he is paying for it, and there is nothing you can do to fix that."

Rod looked around. "Don't you ever mention my Father again, and if I hear one more thing about my Father from you or anyone, I swear to God they will get paid off. You hear me you little shrimp?"

Martek could see the fear in Eric's eyes, and the anger about to arise; yet Eric was still too weak to do anything about it. He knew that if Eric didn't do anything, Rod would. Martek hesitated at first, but something sparked inside of him.

"Hey Rod."

Rod looked over to him.

"What do you want pal?" Rod said in an intimidating manner.

"Why don't you just forget this crap about your parents and leave him alone. He didn't do anything and for you to pick on someone smaller than you, well that makes you look that much smaller."

Rod was furious. He walked to the side of Eric and got right into Martek's face.

"What in the hell did you just say to me shrimp?"

Martek stood there silent. The crowd around was nervous, as Martek was in serious trouble. The last time someone stood up to Rod, they were canned, wedged, and lastly beaten down. That person is still on a limp from that horrible day. Martek remembered that day well, and he knew that Rod had to get a taste of his own medicine one day. Martek got angry.

"Don't call me a shrimp buddy. I am not just some kid you are going to pick on and get away with it."

Rod Laughed. "This guy thinks he can take me on!" He yelled to the crowd. "So you think you are tough huh?"

Rod took his forefinger and pressed it on Martek's chest to nudge him back. Martek was already feeling the blood rush through his veins; his eyes were burning into Rod's. The crowd started to chant the words 'fight', out toward Rod and Martek.

"Come on you little shrimp, let's go." Rod pushed Martek a step back. "You wanted to stand up to me, now you are going to get it."

Martek felt all of his anger rushing into his head, and without notice, he lost control.

"Don't call me shrimp!" Martek screamed to Rod.

With so much anger built up inside of him, Martek pushed Rod so hard that he fell backwards down the stairs and onto the ground at the bottom of the stairs. Rod quickly got back up. The crowd was now silent and gasping at what they had just seen.

"Alright you little prick, you want some? Now you're gonna get it."

Rod ran up to the stairs and grabbed Martek by the collar of his shirt lifting him up into the air, and against the wall behind him. Martek lost a lot of his breath from the force of the wall. Rod pulled his fist back as far as he could.

"This is going to teach you not to mess with people bigger than you; you ungrateful little bastard."

Just as Rod was about to strike Martek, a voice echoed through the air.

"Rodney James Burns!" A voice said.

Rod looked behind him and saw the school Deputy standing there. Deputy Hampton was just as big as Rod, but a lot older and smarter. Not to mention, Deputy Hampton was the school deputy and knew exactly how Rod behaved and would put him away in an instant.

"You put him down right now or you're coming with me downtown."

Rod looked back at Martek with burning eyes. Both of them were breathing hard. He put Martek slowly back down onto his feet and let his shirt go.

"You just made the biggest mistake of your life pal." Rod said.

"Yeah you would think so wouldn't you...? Pal."

Martek said back.

Deputy Hampton walked up to both of them.

"Come on you two; let's go see what Principal Kosh has to say about this."

Deputy Hampton, Martek, and Rod walked through the crowd to the school office. Many of the students were patting Martek on the back and cheering him on. Martek had been the first person ever to physically stand up to Rod Burns, and that was a milestone in Riverdale High School history.

Inside of the office, Martek and Rod were seated just outside of the Principal's office. They both sat glaring at one another. The Deputy saw that they needed to cool off or someone was going to end up doing something they would later regret.

"Alright you two, cool it." The Deputy said.

Martek and Rod cooled down a bit, and just sat back in their chairs waiting for their turn. Principal Kosh was on an important phone call, however he sounded extremely upset about something. What ever it was, it didn't sound good at all.

Deputy Hampton looked at Rod.

"Rod, why do you have to pick on people? You know you are turning just like your Dad. Do you know that? And if you are proud of that, I'll be glad to put you where he is." He said.

Rod looked up at the Deputy and shook his head left and right.

When the call was over, Principal Kosh hung up the phone and walked around his desk to go see Martek and Rod. When he came to the doorway, he looked at Rod and shook his head. He then looked at Martek and raised an eyebrow of curiosity.

"Alright, I'll take it from here. Thanks Deputy." Principal Kosh said. "You two, in my office now."

Martek and Rod got up and walked into the office. The Deputy walked back outside to where the students were just finishing up on their lunch.

Principal Kosh closed the door behind him and looked at both of them.

"You two have a seat right there." He pointed at the two chairs at the front of his desk.

Martek and Rod took a seat and waited for the Principal to walk to his chair at the other side of the desk. When the Principal sat down on his chair, he began to speak.

"So… I heard that there was a fight at lunch. Tell me... Who started it?"

"Martek did." Rod said quickly.

Martek looked over at Rod.

"No I didn't, he lied to you."

"Enough you two; Rod, you go first. What happened today at lunch? What was so important that all of the students on campus *had* to get up and watch some measly old fight?"

"Look! Martek started it by insulting my Dad okay." Rod said in an angry tone.

"Okay, now Martek. Why did you insult his Father?"

"I didn't insult his Dad. He threatened my friend Eric Morris because Eric's parents are cops, and they threw his Dad in jail. Rod told Eric he would see him at lunch, and Rod started it by coming up to Eric and starting something. I was involved because I am not going to see my friend get beat up unfairly. So yes, I did step in to protect my friend. That is no crime at all either."

Rod sat there looking at Martek in a very upsetting stare. He began to crack his knuckles.

"Rodney Burns!" Principal Kosh screamed out.

Rod jolted upright and looked over at Principal

Kosh.

"You know Rod, in all my years at this school you have been one big problem. I am talking about from start to now; you have barely any good record on you. In freshman year, you put a cherry bomb in the toilets in both the men and women's restrooms. You threw balls of paper at teachers who had their backs turned. You beat up a countless amount of students here. You were suspended several times. Shall I go on?"

A long pause.

"You know Rod, I believe Martek. I believe that what he told me is exactly what did happen and I am not a bit surprised. In fact, how would you like it if I decided to tell you that you are no longer a part of the football team?"

"What? You can't do that!" Rod's eyes widened.

"Oh yes I can Rod, but I am not going to. In fact I will cut you a deal. Your senior year is just about up. You have a couple more months left and you're out. The deal is this… If you can go without doing anything wrong from now until graduation, you can stay on the football team and be credited by it. If I find out that you cause one more problem on my campus, I'll make sure you graduate at this school without any sports and any credit. Your name will disappear off of the popular pole faster than you can say anything. Do we have a deal?"

"Well… Okay, deal."

"Good choice. Now, you sadly will be staying after school in detention for provoking this incident."

"That's not fair. What about Martek?"

"Martek didn't start this fight, you did. So in turn Rod, you will go back to class right now, and I expect you to be in detention after school today. You are dismissed…"

Rod got up off of his chair and walked out of the office, Martek was about to get up when Principal Kosh stopped him,

"Martek, stay a bit. I would like to ask you something."

"Uh… Sure I can do that." Martek said sitting back down.

"I understand that it is your birthday pretty soon. Being the school Principal I hear everything that goes around on campus. Now, I heard that you are having a party. I hope that it is a good one and that you have a great birthday."

"Thanks." Martek said.

Principal Kosh saw a small shrug on Martek. "What's the matter?"

"Oh nothing, I just… Well I haven't told all of my friends about the party, and I have some invitations that I can't give out because I haven't seen most of them today."

"I see. Well, you could give me the invitations, and I will call up your friends and have them come up to my office and pick them up. Did you want to do that?"

"Are you serious?" Martek asked in a shocked tone.

"Of course I am serious. Let's see those invitations, and I'll send you back to class, and call your friends up to the office to get their invitations."

Martek opened up his backpack and pulled out his invitations. Each invitation had the first and last name on the front. Principal Kosh was given the invitations and he set them in front of him on the desk.

"Consider this somewhat of a birthday gift from me."

"Okay. And again, thank you Principal Kosh."

"No problem." He said giving Martek the hall pass. "Now go to class and have yourself a great birthday and weekend. I'll be seeing you later."

Martek took the hall pass and walked out of the

office and to his class. When he was walking to class, he heard each of his friend's names being called out on the loud speaker. Of course it sounded like they were in trouble. It was said if a student has to report to the Principal's office, that student was in trouble. Martek thought it was pretty funny. Nonetheless, he walked to his class with a big smile on his face.

At the end of the school day, the bell rang. The halls that were once empty and desolate were now crowded and over-run by students everywhere. Among all of the students were Martek and Eric, who were walking to the bus zone to go home. Everyone was patting Martek on the shoulder, and looking at him in a weird way.

"Dude Martek, you're a celebrity!" Eric said.

"A celebrity? All I did was get into one small fight, it was nothing. Really it wasn't."

"Yeah well you saved my hide, thanks."

"No problem, you would have done the same for me."

"Yeah you are right I would. How did it feel?"

"How did it feel? It felt pretty sweet. When it all came down to it, I wasn't scared of him at all."

"That's good to hear."

Just then, Ashley and her friends walked by Martek and Eric. Ashley was a very pretty blonde hair blue eyed girl. She had a great heart, and was the leader of the Junior Varsity Cheer Squad. She was different though because she wasn't like all of the other cheer leaders, who had sex and partied all the time. She was a down to Earth girl with a great personality. She was also short, and Martek had an unbelievable crush on her. Ashley hardly ever talked to Martek. He thought that she just didn't think he existed at times.

"Hey Martek." A voice came from the side.

Martek looked to his side and saw that it was

Ashley who had said hello. Shocked that she spoke to him, all he did was smile and say hello back.

"…Hi…" He smiled.

"I just wanted to say that I thought it was nice for what you did at lunch. You're really sweet." Ashley said.

"Thanks. It was nothing." He said memorized in her eyes.

"Ashley…" Her friend said. "Ashley let's go before the bus leaves us." Her friend Jennifer said holding her by the arm and dragging her back to the bus.

"Okay well… Bye Martek. I'll see you later, and have a good weekend."

"Okay. Bye Ashley, you too."

"Man. Did Ashley Holt just talk to you?" Eric said in shock.

"I… I think so." Martek said still looking at her as she walked away.

Eric smacked Martek in the back of his head.

"Snap out of it dude!" Eric said laughing.

"What? What did I do?"

They both laughed.

Eric and Martek walked to their bus and boarded it. The bus driver was sitting there at his chair just as Martek walked up the steps.

"So Martek." The bus driver said. "I heard what happened buddy."

"You did?"

"Yeah, the entire bus is talking about it." He said pointing back.

As Martek continued through the isle to his seat, cheers and claps from students everywhere began. Everyone cheered Martek on for standing up to Rod Burns. Pats on the back were given and believe it or not, a few asked for his autograph.

"Wow, you're a celebrity Martek!" Eric shouted behind him.

Martek and Eric found John and Druid sitting just ahead toward the back of the bus. They both sat next to them, and talked about what happened at lunch.

"Hey Martek, hey Eric." Druid said.

"What's up man?" Martek asked.

John stepped in. "Hey Martek, what was it like standing up to Rod? Did you get into any trouble?"

"It was nothing really. Standing up to Rod was nothing at all, and he was the only one to get in trouble."

"You mean you didn't get in trouble?" Druid asked.

"Nope, Rod was the one that was eating dirt in that office, not me. That made me glad. The Principal did take my invitations for the party tomorrow and gave them to the ones that are coming tomorrow. I hope everyone can make it. I was going to pass out the invitations at lunch, but that thing happened so I didn't."

"Yeah some of the people got those invitations. I talked to a few of them just before I got onto the bus." John said.

The rows of buses were filled with all of the students as they rolled off of the school driveway and to their destinations. The bus outside the left side window right next to Martek's bus was full of students, who were hollering and cheering at Martek. Martek looked over and waved and nodded his head. He wasn't really into this attention, and all because of one fight; he was the new school celebrity. He thought about after the weekend on Monday and Rod. He wondered what would happen to him, or Eric. Of course, there was a party tomorrow, and Martek wasn't going to let one little thing ruin it.

The bus rolled over the Santa Ana River Bridge, and the view was great. He could see the sparkling waters of the river reflecting the sunlight. The skies were a pure blue, and the sun was warming up the air as it came closer to the Summer Season.

Just past the river was a road to the right that led to John's neighborhood. The bus turned on that road and headed into a rather nice neighborhood. The homes were all one story homes but the area was very peaceful, not as rich as Martek's area though.

"Almost at my stop." John said as he gathered his stuff together.

Martek noticed that Druid was getting his stuff together too. He turned and noticed that Eric was also getting his stuff together.

"What's going on? Are both of you guys getting off at the same bus stop?" Martek asked.

"Yeah, they are both spending the night at my house. This way we can all go to your party in the morning together." John said.

"Oh okay, that sounds like a good idea. I'll talk to you all later on tonight or something."

"Sounds good buddy, we'll see you later." Druid said.

The bus came up to the bus stop and stopped. Students stood up and headed to the exit. John, Druid, and Eric got up and walked to the front of the bus, and were out of sight. Martek sat back in his seat and waved to them as they crossed the street. The bus doors shut, and they left the bus stop. Minutes later down the road, he was dropped off at his own bus stop.

CHAPTER 3

Martek got to his house. He went to the mail box and checked for mail. He grabbed letter after letter and looked through them, but found nothing but bills.

"I never get anything good." He said.

He walked up to the front door and turned the doorknob, but found out that it was locked.

"That's strange." He said. "Good thing I brought the key along.

He reached into his pocket and pulled out the house key and inserted it into the keyhole. When he got inside he looked around the house to see if his Mom was home.

"Mom, are you in here? Long pause. "Hey Mom!"

Martek looked everywhere inside of the house but couldn't find his Mom anywhere. He walked to the garage door and opened it, realizing that his Mom's car wasn't even in there.

"Guess she's not home." He said as he shut the

garage door.

He went down the hall and into his room. He threw his backpack down on the ground and headed to his computer. Being a Friday, Martek had no homework to do, and he was excited about his birthday being tomorrow. The party was something that he was definitely looking forward to.

He signed online and checked his email. Martek had over fifty emails, which most were junk any ways. He searched through his emails and found a few from his friends. He saw one from his friend Stephen, who he invited to the party; which read -

Martek,

How's it going man? As for me, nothing much. I got your invitation to the party and I just wanted to let you know that I'll be there. Thanks for the invite and I'll see you tomorrow! Have a good day!
        Your friend, Stephen
        AKA STEVE MAN

Martek opened up the next email.

Hey Martek!

What's up dude? Thanks for the invitation man. I'll be there tomorrow just to let you know. Thanks again!

Robert

He opened the next email

Alright Martek! A party? That's awesome bro! Thanks for the invite. It was weird getting it from the school principal, but oh well. I'll be there for sure! See you tomorrow!

Your friend, Jason McCool

He saw one last email and opened it.

Hey buddy ole' pal! What's happening? Me not much. Hey I got that invite from the office and I'll be there. Such short notice huh? You are lucky I had an open weekend this weekend LOL! Anyways, I'll talk to you later... No wait, I'll SEE YOU LATER!!

From Chris

"Alright, that's four so far. So I got these four, John, Druid, and Eric. Seven so far isn't bad at all. That's more than half the people I invited, only a few left."

Martek received an online instant message from Druid.

DruidMaster: Hey Buddy, glad to see you online. What's going down?

GreatMartek: Hey Druid, not much. I just got a few emails from a few more people saying that they are going to the party tomorrow.

DruidMaster: Awesome dude! Who are the ones that said they are going to be there?

GreatMartek: It was Stephen, Robert, Jason, and Chris.

DruidMaster: Robert is going? That's cool!

GreatMartek: You bet! So what are you doing right now?

DruidMaster: Come on, you know what I always do online. I am kicking the living hell out of other online players on Counter-Struck

GreatMartek: LOL. That's funny. You and that game dude I swear.

DruidMaster: What? This game rocks, you should jump in right now and kick some terrorist ass!

DruidMaster: You have the game don't you?

GreatMartek: Yeah I have the game. You know I have that game we played before and you kept finding me and shooting me.

DruidMaster: Ah yes, I remember that. Good ole' days weren't they?

DruidMaster: So are you going to jump in or not? Jump in so I can find you and kill you, hehe.

GreatMartek: Yeah I bet you want me to jump in so you can find me and keep shooting me. I'm not stupid LOL.

DruidMaster: Nah, you aren't stupid. Just you need to get in the game right now. We'll be on the same team. I promise I won't kill you!

Just then, Martek got an email from an address he didn't recognize. That e-mail's subject was Hi Martek.

He opened it.

Hey Martek,

It's Ashley, hope everything is doing good. I got your email from my friend, who is friends with one of your friends so I hope you don't mind. I just wanted to say hey and that I hope that you are doing better than you did at lunch. I saw what you did for your friend and that was awesome. You are one brave guy let me tell you. From Rod's size to yours, I can see who has the bigger guts. Any ways, Happy Birthday. I heard that it was your birthday tomorrow, and I hope you have a good birthday! I am going to get going. This is my email so if you want, email me back and let me know how things are going! Talk to you later. I am having a girl's sleep over party tonight, and we just ordered pizza and its here so I'll talk to you later! Take care Martek!

XOXO Ashley

Martek was shocked and couldn't blink or anything. He was shocked that Ashley had emailed him; she actually notices him. Martek replied back to Ashley's email.

Dear Ashley

It's Martek, thanks for the email it was great. Its okay about you getting my email, I don't mind at all! I am doing much better now ever since lunch. Lunch wasn't exactly the best day ever but I feel tons better. I am just tired of Rod and his macho attitude and someone had to do it sometime. Thanks for the happy birthday. I'll be seventeen tomorrow and man time is flying past. Hope you are having a good party tonight and the pizza

sounds good, I wish I was there to grab a slice! LOL!
Anyways, I'll talk to you later. Email me at anytime you
want! Take care too!

> *Later,*
> *Martek*

Martek sent the email and received an instant
message from Druid, who he forgot he was still talking
to.

> *DruidMaster: Hey Martek, what are you doing?*
> *Are you there?*

> *DruidMaster: MARTEK! Where'd you go?*

> *GreatMartek: Oh Sorry man! I got some email*
> *and I just emailed her back.*

> *DruidMaster. There you are. An email? Her? So*
> *it was a she huh? Well who is the girl?*

> *GreatMartek: You wouldn't believe it if I told you.*

> *DruidMaster: Try me. Come on, who was it?*

> *GreatMartek: It was Ashley Holt.*

> *DruidMaster: You're right. I don't believe you.*

> *GreatMartek: LOL. Well believe it because she*
> *emailed me two minutes ago so HA!*

> *DruidMaster: Alright, alright, no bragging buddy.*

> *DruidMaster: So how about that game?*

GreatMartek: Alright let me load it up first.

DruidMaster: Great! Prepare to die… I mean… Prepare to survive. ☺

GreatMartek: Die? We'll see about that one buddy. ☺

Martek was about to put the game CD in, when his mom walked into the house.

"Martek, I'm home!" His Mom shouted.

"Coming Mom!"

GreatMartek: Man, my Mom just got home. Sounds like she went to the store so I got to get going. I'll play the game later. Is that cool?

DruidMaster: Oh… That's okay, we'll play later on. I'll talk to you later.

GreatMartek: Okay, thanks, talk to you later. Bye!

DruidMaster: Later buddy.

Martek quickly signed offline and rushed out to the kitchen to meet up with his Mom. He saw her putting groceries on the counter in the kitchen.

"Hey Mom. I see you went shopping."

"Hey Martek, How was your day?"

"It was interesting enough. Just can't wait for tomorrow that's all."

"That's good. Speaking of tomorrow, I bought a whole bunch of goodies for the party. Let's see; I bought Popcorn, Candy, Soda, Chips, Dip, Salsa, Cheese Dip, and I'll be making the cake later on tonight."

"Wow! This is so great! The party is going to be awesome. Thanks Mom!" He gave his Mom a big hug.

"You're welcome Hun. Can you do me a favor? Go out to my car and get the last of the groceries for me, lock up the car, and bring the groceries in and set them here on the counter please."

"Sure Mom." Martek said while heading to the car.

He walked to the car and got the last of the groceries, locked it up, and went back in. He dropped the groceries where his Mom told him to put them.

"Thank you Hun."

"You're welcome."

"Now let's see. I was thinking about making some good steak tonight, but I thought it would be nice to take you out to dinner tonight."

"Really?" He said excitedly.

"Of course, I thought we could go to the Rock Star Grill. Does that sound good?"

"That sounds like a great idea! Wow, thanks Mom!"

"Great, I am going to get ready and you should too. I'll be ready to leave in about ten minutes."

"Okay Mom."

Martek rushed back to his room to get ready. He didn't need much else other than a thin long sleeve shirt. When Martek was completely ready, he went to the kitchen table and sat down to wait for his Mom. When his Mom came out, he got up and both of them went out to the car.

While they were driving down the freeway toward downtown, they heard a weather statement on the radio. Martek turned the volume up so they could hear what the news was talking about.

"The National Weather Service has issued the possibility for severe weather Tuesday Night. This storm system is a rather dangerous system giving it a potential for heavy rain, deadly lightning, severe winds, and even the threat for tornadoes. While right now we can't tell whether a tornado is possible in this system, we have reason to believe it is. One of our sources comes from Meteorologist Kevin Martin of the Ontario Weather Service. Kevin you're on."

"This is Kevin Martin of the Ontario Weather Service. The latest weather models pose a threat for the Riverdale County areas of tornadoes and deadly thunderstorms. Winds could exceed over sixty miles an hour and given the values of this storm, I am putting the Entire Riverdale County on a Severe Thunderstorm Watch and a Tornado Watch Tuesday Night starting at 5pm and ending at 10pm. The area that is most likely to see a tornado is South Riverdale just east of the Riverdale Hills. The Thunderstorms will move over the Riverdale Hills and inland threatening everything east of the hills. For more information, tune in later for any updates."

And there you have it. Kevin Martin of the Ontario Weather Service has forecasted both a Severe Thunderstorm Watch and a Tornado Watch for the greater South County of Riverdale City. Kevin is known and respected for his detailed weather forecasts and mostly extremely accurate on all of his forecasts. For more local information, visit www.ontarioweatherservice.com"

"Wow Mom, did you hear that? Sounds like a bad storm headed this way next week."

"Yeah, that is unusual. We never get any bad weather out here. It would be something if we did though because we sure need that rain."

"You said it. I heard something about Tornadoes. You don't think we'll have tornadoes. Do you?" Martek asked in a concerned tone.

"No, I don't think it will get that bad. It never does, although this is the first time hearing anything about a tornado in this area so I don't know."

"I hope not. I mean… Seeing Thunderstorms would be really nice for a change, but no tornado."

"Yeah, I'll take anything but that tornado."

"So who is that Kevin guy?"

"People at the station are trying to figure out how he nails a lot of this weather. He isn't an actual Meteorologist and he is only twenty-one years old."

"What makes him so famous about the weather?"

"He uses these neat formulas to forecast his own weather, and owns his own weather service in Ontario just north of here."

"That's pretty cool. So since he is mostly right on the forecasts… Does that mean he is right about the Tornado?"

"I don't know. It scares me to hear Kevin mentioning an actual tornado in this area though."

"Yeah I know, that is crazy isn't it."

They got off the freeway and headed off to Main Street. They turned right onto Second Street and then left onto Main Street and headed about a mile down the road. Just to the left was the Rock Star Grill. They pulled into the driveway and parked in the parking lot.

"Alright, I am so hungry I could eat a horse right about now." Martek said.

"I don't think they serve horses here."

They both laughed.

Both of them got out of the car and entered the restaurant. When they went in, they were greeted but the Host.

"Hello, and welcome to the Rock Star Grill, How many?"

"Just two." His Mom said.

"Right this way, please."

Martek and his Mom followed the Host to a nice table right next to the window, overlooking the Northern Mountains of Riverdale. They sat down.

"Will this table be okay?" The Host asked.

"Oh yes, this table is great. Thank you." Sarah said.

"Very good, your waiter will be with you momentarily."

"Okay." Sarah smiled.

The Host walked back to the front of the restaurant to greet other guests.

"Wow, this is nice Mom, thank you."

"Hey it's no problem."

A second later, the waiter came to greet Martek and Sarah.

"Hello, I am Antonio. I'll be your waiter. Can I start you out with anything to drink?" He said while placing menus on the table for Martek and Sarah.

"I'll take a Lemon Ice Tea." Sarah said.

"An excellent choice... And how about you, sir?"

"I'll have a Sprite please."

"Very good. Are you ready to order?"

"No I think we'll need a few more minutes." Sarah said politely as she smiled.

"Order when you are ready; let me get your drinks."

The Waiter walked back around the corner into kitchen to get the drinks.

"Wow Mom, he seems like a nice waiter."

"Yes, he does."

"So what are you going to order?" Martek asked.

"Honestly, I don't know. There is so much here that looks so good, I may need to sample all of them." Sarah said as she held her stomach.

Both laughed.

"You know they have a sampler." He said pointing down at her menu.

She smiled.

"So they have. I think I might have that. Do you know what you are going to get?" She asked.

"I have my eyes set on this Teriyaki Chicken. It comes with a soup or salad, and French fries or baked potato."

"That sounds really good to me, I might have that too. My sampler doesn't come with the Salad and the French fries." She laughed.

"You copy cat!" Martek said laughing along.

"Hey. Who's paying for your meal buddy?"

"You are."

"That's what I thought. I didn't think you wanted to do dishes here." She smiled.

The Waiter came to the table and gave them their drinks.

"Here's an Ice Tea for you, and here is a Sprite for you. Have you two decided on what you would like to order?"

"Actually we have." Martek said.

"Very good, let's start with the lady."

"Oh okay. I would like to have the Teriyaki Chicken dinner."

"Another excellent choice. Would you care for a Soup or Salad?"

"Salad please."

"And what kind of Salad dressing?"

"I'll take Ranch."

"Very good. And Baked Potato or French Fries?"

"Baked Potato, please."

"Okay. And for you sir?"

"I'll take the exact same thing, except I'd like French Fries instead of a baked potato please."

"Very good. Is there anything else I can get you?"

Martek looked around.

"Not that I see here. Thank you."

"If you need anything, please let me know."

The Waiter walked away with their order and took it to the kitchen.

Several hours later, Sarah and Martek finished with their dinner. She was given the bill, in which she paid for. As they were leaving, she set the tip on the table and walked off.

"Thank you." The Host said.

"No, thank you. It was great, have a good night." Sarah said.

"You're welcome, you do the same."

Sarah and Martek walked out of the restaurant and headed to the car. She unlocked the car doors and they both got in.

"Thanks Mom, I am stuffed. That was really good."

"You're welcome. I am glad you liked it, I did as well."

Sarah started the car and they drove back home happily satisfied.

When they arrived at the house, Martek walked down the hall to his room, while Sarah walked to the living room and sat down to watch some television.

Martek got into his room and shut the door. He went to his computer and sat down at the desk to sign online. When he was signed online, he was greeted by John and Druid.

SirJohn: Hey Martek! What's up?

GreatMartek: Hey John how's everything?

SirJohn: Everything is fine so far. Eric's parents said that it was okay if he can go to your party tomorrow afternoon.

SirJohn: He is also staying the night here so we three can go to your house at the same time.

GreatMartek: Oh wow, that is cool, thanks for telling me. I am happy to hear that.

Martek checked his mail and saw that he got a couple of emails. One was from his friend Brian, and the other was from Ashley. He checked the first one from Brian.

Hey Martek,

This is Brian. Ill be able to make it tomorrow to your party. I'll be there at the time it starts. Thanks for the invite I can't wait man. Peace out.

-Brian

"Awesome." Martek said. "Looks like Brian's going after all."

He opened up the next one. This was from Ashley.

Martek,

Yeah that is what he deserved. I never liked Rod. I am glad you did something about it. The pizza was great and the party is really fun. Hope your night is going great and you have a blast at your party tomorrow. Have a good night Martek, sleep good!

Always,
Ashley

PS - Would have been nice if you came over and had some pizza with us!!! ;)

Martek's jaw dropped.

"Wow, she said it would be nice if I was over there!" He gave a big grin.

SirJohn: Martek, where'd you go?

GreatMartek: Sorry guys, I was just reading up on emails. Brian is going to the party.

SirJohn: That's good news! Did he email you?

GreatMartek: Yes, I just got one from him tonight. So he is going to be here tomorrow.

SirJohn: That's good. So are you feeling better ever since that thing at lunch?

GreatMartek: Yeah, I am feeling a lot better. The more I think about it, the more he deserved it. So honestly nothing can make me happier than to know he got his.

SirJohn: That's good thinking. We all agree over here.

"Martek!" His Mom yelled from down the hall.
"Yeah Mom?"
"You've got a phone call!"
"Okay, I'm coming!"

GreatMartek: Guys, I'll be right back. I have a phone call.

SirJohn: We'll be here.

Martek got up and ran down the hall to the phone. He grabbed the phone from the kitchen and started talking.

"Hello?" Martek said.

"Hey Martek, it's me Kevin."

"Hey Kevin, what's up?"

"Oh nothing much, I tried to call earlier today but no one was home."

"Oh I'm sorry about that; I was at dinner with my Mom."

"That's okay. I just wanted to let you know that I got the invitation from the Principal today and I can go to your party."

"That's awesome to hear, I am glad you are able to make it."

"Yeah... I have Just one thing, Martek."

"What's that?"

"Next time try not to have me called up to the office, which scared the living hell out of me."

They both laughed.

"Okay I won't. So you know how to get to my house?"

"Yeah, the directions on the invite seem very clear. I'll be able to find it."

"Great, so I'll see you tomorrow morning then."

"You got it, see you tomorrow."

"Alright. Bye Kevin."

"Later."

Martek got off the phone and hung it back on the hook. He raced to the living room and told his Mom who was coming.

"Hey Mom, Brian and Kevin just let me know that they are coming to my party tomorrow."

"Oh that's good to hear."

Martek raced back to his room and sat at the computer.

GreatMartek: Okay guys, I'm back.

SirJohn: Hey.

GreatMartek: Hi. So anyway, it is getting close to that time. I should get to sleep so I can wake up for that party tomorrow. I'll see you all tomorrow.

SirJohn: Okay dude, we'll see you later. Night.

GreatMartek: Night guys.

Martek signed offline and yelled Goodnight to his Mom. He got ready for bed and set his alarm. He turned off the light and rolled to his side and fell into a deep sleep.

Martek woke up lying on his back in the middle of a forest. He got up noticing that his vision was a bit blurry. As he was looking around, he noticed that he was wearing some sort of suit or costume; looking at his gloves. Suddenly, a dark shadow engulfed him. He turned around only to see a dark figured silhouette standing on top of a hill covering the full moon. Martek stared at the dark shadow and its eyes glowed bright yellow in color.

Martek shook violently as he awakened. He looked around and realized that it was only a dream.

"It must have been a dream." He said.

He was safe in his room. He lied back down on his back and wiped the sweat off of his face, looking over to the clock.

"It's only three; I still have several more hours to go." He rolled back over and fell back asleep.

CHAPTER 4

At eight in the morning, Martek's alarm went off. He hit his alarm clock and the alarm turned off. He was about to fall back asleep when he realized what day it was today.

"It's my birthday!" Martek said as he jumped out of bed.

He rushed out of his room to see his Mom already decorating the house.

"Happy Birthday Son." His Mom said.

She gave him a big hug.

"Thanks Mom! Finally one more year to go and I'll be eighteen."

"Yeah, you are growing up."

"Mom, I'm going to go get ready and check my mail to see if I got anything else from my friends."

"Okay, I'll see you when you get back. If you need me, you know where to find me."

Martek ran down the hall and into his room. He signed online and found out that he got an email from Ashley.

Dear Martek,

I just wanted to wish you a Happy 17th Birthday today and that I hope you have a great day! HAPPY BIRTHDAY!!

Always,
Ashley

"That was nice of her to write to me. I'll have to email her and tell her thank you."

Dear Ashley,

This is Martek. Thanks for wishing me a Happy Birthday. It means a lot to me. I hope you have a fun weekend and I'll talk to you later. Thanks again!

Martek

Martek sent the email and sat back in his chair with a smile on his face.

He got up and quickly showered to get ready for the party. When he was ready, he rushed out to help his Mom with anything she needed help on. She mostly got all the decorations out so there wasn't much else to do. He got the snacks together in individual bowls and set them on the table. The house looked great. There were blue ribbons everywhere, balloons that said Happy Birthday on them, and much more.

It was just about ten o'clock in the morning; the party should start very soon.

The doorbell rang.

"I'll get it Mom!"

Martek raced to the door and opened it to see who

it was.

"Hey Martek, Happy Birthday!"

"Hey Stephen, glad you could make it."

Stephen came in, along with the gift he was carrying.

"The present can go in the living room." Martek said.

Stephen was about the same age as Martek. He was a blonde haired wimp, and about six feet tall.

Stephen took the gift and set it by the fireplace in the living room by the kitchen. He saw Sarah.

"Well hello Stephen. How are you?"

"Hi Ms. Majestic, I am doing fine. How are you?"

"Fine, thank you. Hey Martek. I am going to be heading to my room right now. Have fun and let me know when you guys are ready to order those pizzas."

"That sounds great, thanks!" Martek said.

Sarah walked down the hall and into her room out of sight.

"Well Stephen, the snacks are over here and we are having pizza for lunch. Everyone should be coming soon but you are the first one."

"Sweet."

Then the doorbell rang again.

Martek walked over to the door and opened it. It was John, Druid, and Eric.

"Hey guys, come on in!"

They all come in, and a big decorated box that Druid was holding caught Martek's eye.

"Hey Martek, where do I put this thing?" Druid asked.

"Is that a present?"

"No it's a box, of course it's a gift to you. It is your birthday." Druid laughed.

"Oh okay, it goes in the living room by the

fireplace." Martek said laughing.

Everybody headed to the dining room table and saw all of the delicious snacks. They started to eat the candy and other goodies.

"So I see Stephen beat us here. Let's kill him." Druid said pointing at Stephen.

"Hey you know me guys, I am always early." Stephen said.

"I say its better late then never." John said.

They all laugh.

The doorbell rang.

Martek rushed to it to see who it was. He opened the door.

"Hey Martek!" Chris and Jason said.

"Hey guys, come in, thanks for coming."

"Happy Birthday." They said as they came in.

"Thanks guys. The gifts go in the living room over there by the fireplace."

Chris and Jason walked in and set the gifts by the fireplace. They came into the dining room and were met by everyone else. They greeted one another and dug into the snacks as well.

After a while, Kevin and Brian arrived, Robert was last.

When everyone was around the dining room table, Martek got up and stood at the far end of the table.

"Attention... Attention everyone!" He yelled.

Everyone quieted down and looked up at Martek.

"Alright everyone, there are going to be rules to this party."

"Oh come on Martek! Who needs rules?" Druid shouted out.

"Calm down guys, I only have one rule; and that is to have fun."

Everyone quieted down and smiled.

"Oh in that case, that's more like it." Druid said.

"Yeah I have to agree, I like that rule." Robert added.

"My Mom is ordering Pizza for lunch. We are getting three large pizzas with two toppings on each one. My question is what kind of toppings do you guys like?"

Druid stepped up to the plate.

"Alright everyone likes pepperoni so we are going to assume that we will get that." Druid said.

"Hey! What about Hawaiian?" Stephen stepped in and said.

"Hawaiian is a good one." Martek said pointing. "Is there anything else?"

"I know. What about those kinds where you have the BBQ chicken and the sauce on it. That is really good pizza, and if anyone has tried it they'll know what I mean."

"Yes, that is good I'll have to agree." Martek agreed. "Okay, so is everyone okay with this choice?" Martek said.

Everyone agreed.

"Alright, I'm going to go let my Mom know what to order. Druid, since you brought the CD's that makes you today's music man."

"Already a step ahead of you bro." Druid said.

Martek walked down the hall to let his Mom know what they decided on.

Druid walked to the big stereo system at the corner of the family room and put in a CD that had the best rock music around. The music started to play and everyone started to dance, sing, and rock out with music. They all dug into all the mass variety of snacks that were on the dining room table.

Martek knocked on his Mom's door. She opened the door.

"Did you all decide what you want me to order?"

"Yeah, we did. We want one with pepperoni, the

other Hawaiian, and the last one is the BBQ Chicken."

"Ok, I'll go ahead and order that for you guys. Give it about thirty to forty-five minutes."

"Alright, thanks Mom."

Martek headed back to the party and could see that everyone was enjoying themselves. He saw most of the group had relocated to the corner couch section. He got closer and could see his friends huddled around in a circle on the floor.

"All I can say is you should have been there when Rod and Martek fought. He literally gave him a bit of his own medicine." Eric said.

"No, I don't think it was a bit of his medicine, I think it was the whole thing; the whole freaking bottle." Druid said.

They all laughed.

A voice came from above them.

"Actually guys, it wasn't the whole thing. I'd say it was the whole enchilada."

They all looked up to see Martek standing above them.

"Yeah, you bet it was!" John said.

Martek made his way into the circle and sat down to join in on the discussion.

After roughly thirty-five minutes, the door bell rang.

"Pizza!" Someone shouted out.

Sarah rushed out of her room and to the front door. She could tell she was not alone; everyone was following her like hungry zombies on a rampage. She opened the door.

"Hello, that will be thirty-four fifty please." The pizza man said.

Sarah handed the pizza man two twenty dollar bills.

"Here, keep the change."

"Thank you very much."

Just as Sarah was about to take the pizzas from the man's hand, all of Martek's friends one by one took the boxes of pizza and ran back inside. Sarah and the Pizza man laughed.

"Wow, they must be hungry." He said.

"Yeah, teenagers will be teenagers I suppose."

Sarah smiled and closed the door. She walked past the kitchen and into the dining room table where all the commotion was. Everyone was ravaging the pizza boxes like they were pieces of silk. Before all of the pizza was gone, she quickly grabbed a slice of pizza and ran down the hall back to her room.

Everyone laughed.

"Wow dude, your Mom looked hungry." Druid said.

"Yeah, she did." Martek laughed.

When everyone had their pizzas and drinks, Martek went over to the front of the room near the television and asked for everyone's attention.

"Alright everyone, I decided it would be cool to watch a movie. Since it is my birthday and you all know I enjoy scary movies, we are going to watch a scary movie. I have three movies and all of you let me know which one is the best. I personally have a best, but I want to know what you guys think."

"A scary movie? My Mom told me not to watch those things." Stephen said with a smile.

Someone from behind the group threw an empty soda can at Stephen.

"Down in front Stephen." A voice said from behind Stephen.

Everyone looked back, and it was Brian who threw the can.

"Hey, it's true. But I'll watch them any way." Stephen said.

"Alright everyone, first choice is Nightmare on Elm Street." Martek shouted.

"Is that the one with that killer doll?" Stephen asked.

Another can was thrown at Stephen.

"Hey, what the heck?" He said.

"Stupid, that is Chucky." Brian said. "The movie is called Child's Play. The one Martek is talking about is with Freddy Krueger in it. This guy gets inside of your dreams and kills you."

"Oh yeah, now I remember." Stephen said.

Not many hands went up on that movie. The only ones were Jason and Kevin who voted on it.

"Alright, second choice is going to be Friday the 13th."

"Oh I like that one." Brian said raising his hand.

Just about four people voted on that movie.

"Okay, the last one is Halloween; which is my favorite."

Martek raised his hand up along with Druid, John, and Stephen.

"Alright, we have a tie, but since it is my birthday we are watching Halloween because Michael Myers is the best, and he will beat Jason any day." He smiled.

"Bring it!" Brian screamed.

Everyone laughed.

Everyone got seated and Martek put the movie in and started it. The previews came on and he fast forwarded it to the feature presentation. The movie opened up with the Halloween Main theme.

"I swear this is the scariest theme song I have ever heard." Martek said.

"Yeah, it is." Stephen said looking around himself, wary on ballistic cans headed his way.

Martek went to the blinds at the window and shut them all the way. He turned down all of the lights, which made the room incredibly scary.

"Do you have to do that?" Stephen said."

"Down in front." Brian said throwing a can at Stephen.

"You know what, If you throw another can at me I'll shove it up your…"

"Hey the movie is starting." John interrupted.

Everyone started to laugh.

A couple of hours passed and the movie was just about over.

"No, don't go upstairs you idiot!" Stephen screamed.

By now Stephen has gotten very much into the movie, he found himself telling the actors to watch out.

"I don't get it. Why do the girls run up the stairs and not out of the front or back door?" Druid said.

"Because, it's a basic horror movie; it wouldn't be a horror movie if it had smart people in it." Brian said.

"Good point." Druid added.

When the movie was over, everyone gave a great applause.

"Classic movie, just classic." Brian said.

"It was a great movie." Stephen said.

"You bet it was; now what?" Chris said.

Martek got up and turned the television off.

"Now, we go to the living room and open up the gifts." Martek said.

Everyone agreed, got up and went over to the living room. Some took seats on the couches, others on the floor. Martek took a seat in between John and Druid on the main couch. Stephen walked over to his present and picked it up; giving it to Martek.

"Here you go. Happy Birthday."

"Thanks Steve."

Martek opened up the card first and read it. After he read it, he opened up the gift and was in shock.

"Oh wow Stephen, this is awesome!"

"I thought you might like it."

"Like it, I love it dude!"

Martek held in his hands the computer game, Counter-Struck 2.

"Yeah buddy, that means I'll be able to play this game version with you and everyone else. Better hope you are prepared pal, it's way better than the first version." Druid said smiling.

"Hey, let me at least get used to it. You've been playing longer than I have." Martek laughed.

Robert gave Martek his present.

Martek opened up the single white envelope, which had thirty dollars inside of it.

"I thought you might want money instead. I didn't know what to get you, so I decided that you could just go and get anything that you might want."

"This is awesome Robert, thank you very much." Martek smiled.

After Martek went through everyone's presents, he thanked them all. The only thing that remained was a very large box at the corner near the fireplace. Druid got up and walked over to the box and picked it up, placing it in front of Martek.

"Happy birthday man; this is from John, Eric, and me."

Martek had to stand up in order to get to the top of the present. The gift stood at least four feet from the ground and about three feet from side to side. He ripped open the gift wrapping and opened up the cardboard box and was amazed. He reached inside and took out a single Laser Tag unit. The box contained ten laser tag units total. This was the Laser Tag 5000, which was one of the rarest toys in the world. Martek was shocked.

"Oh wow! Thanks you guys! Look at all this stuff!"

"Glad you like it man" Druid said.

"Yeah, happy birthday dude." John said.

"Thanks everyone. Wow this is a great birthday. Thank you all for coming."

"It's not over yet. I figured since there are enough people that we should all go out to the Riverdale Hills and play a little laser tag. There is a blue team and a red team, I have the red team, and Martek will take the blue team. What do you say?" Druid said.

Everyone jumped up in excitement.

"Martek that sounds killer, let's do that!" Brian said.

"I'm game." Chris said.

"Alright guys, I'll go let my Mom know where we are going. Let's do that."

Everyone cheered.

Martek ran down the hall way and knocked on his Mom's door.

"Mom, we are going to go out and play laser tag, we'll be back in a few hours. Is that okay?"

"Have fun, I'll see you in a few!" She shouted through the door.

Martek ran back to the living room.

"Alright guys, lets get out of here. Grab your waters, sodas, and anything to drink and we are out of here."

Druid and John closed the box and picked it up.

"We'll pick our teams when we get there." Druid said.

"Alright, let's go guys."

Martek and his friends went out of the front door and walked west down the street that would lead them to the Riverdale Hills.

CHAPTER 5

The afternoon was not that hot at all. In fact, it was quite nice just sitting around seventy-five degrees. The sky was clear, not a cloud in the sky could be seen for miles. Martek and everyone walked down the street to the Riverdale Hills. The hills were only about a mile away, so it wasn't a long walk at all. They all walked in a group talking about who was going to be on whose team.

"I got Martek's team, that's for sure guys." Brian said.

"Hey Brian, we will pick teams when we get there." Martek smiled.

Just about a half hour later, they reached the foot of the hills. The area was fenced off, but the gate was open to have access to the dirt trail that led to the top.

"Alright guys, this is it. All we have to do is go to the top and we are there." Druid said.

They made their way up in a single file line to the top, following the dirt trail. Jason looked behind him and stood there.

"What are you doing Jason? Why did you stop?" Eric asked.

"Check out that view you guys."

Everyone turned around and looked back to see that whole city of Riverdale.

"Wow! You can see everything from up here!"

Martek looked at the sight and just imagined what it would be like to be as free as a bird. He closed his eyes and imagined it all.

"Yeah man, that is some view." He said.

"Alright guys, we are almost there. Just about thirty more feet up and we'll be at the top."

"What's at the top Druid?" Kevin asked.

"You'll see it when we get there." Druid said smiling. "Now let's go guys."

Everyone continued onward to the very top of the hills.

When they reached the top of the hills, everyone rested. Most of them who hadn't been up to the top were extremely surprised at what they were seeing. The land was a large green field, piled with stacks of pine trees, and other such trees on the other side of the field.

Druid stood in front of everyone.

"Alright guys, we made it. The reason why we are going to play laser tag here is because through those trees is a land of many hiding spots and guerilla tactics. Also, if you walk to the middle of this tree patch and to the left or right, you'll run into rock formations that will make perfect bases for each team. Each rock formation is about a half a mile apart from one another, so our laser tag area is roughly a half a mile of coverage. That alone guys is a really great distance and it will make this game more challenging. Are there any questions?"

Brian raised his hand.

"Hey Druid, come on now. What are the teams

going to be?"

"Well Brian, I am going to be in charge of one team; the Red Team. Martek is going to be in charge of the Blue Team. The team leaders are going to be the ones to decide who to pick. Don't worry, we will make it fair."

Druid and Martek stood in front of everyone. They got all of the equipment and sorted it out by color of team. Martek got his stuff together and Druid did the same. After everything was sorted out, Druid went over the rules and how to use the equipment.

"Okay guys, this equipment is a bit easy to use so pay attention. First off, my team will be the Red Team; Martek's will be the Blue Team. Each Team will have their own group radios. Your radios will only communicate back and forth to people on your team. If you are on the red team, you can only talk to someone on the red team. You may not talk to someone on the opposite team, which is the blue team. These radios are designed so you can not communicate with your enemy."

Druid held up a set of headphones.

"These are your headsets. They are used so you can hear communications between your teammates. The volume control is here on the control panel that is strapped to your wrist. The strap is Velcro so it is easy to put on. This button by the volume is the communications button. If you hold it down and talk, your voice will be transmitted. Now, pay attention. If you want hands free so that your group can hear everything that you say without touching any buttons, just flip the hands off switch to the on position. This feature comes in handy if you are in heavy battle and can't get to the button on time. It also lets you observe your surroundings better, so no one can attack you easily. As you can see, there is a wireless laser gun that comes with each of these things. All you do is flip up the on switch, and it will last you two days straight on a full battery. I just charged these things last night, so you won't die in the middle of being shot at."

Everyone laughed.

"The gun is simple, just point and shoot. It also has a very unique feature on it. You can look through the scope on the top to zoom in on your target. This comes in handy when firing at far range. Are there any questions?"

No one raised their hands.

"Okay, so now time for me to go over the rules. Martek is the Blue Team, you will call him Commander Martek. I am Commander Druid, leader of the Red Team. There will be five players per team. Each team will have their own base. The bases are the rock formations north and south of the center of our battle zone. Martek and I will show the teams where the bases are at. The objective of this game will be by defeat. There are two ways to win this game. If one team takes over another team's base by standing at the very top of the rock formation, they win. If every person on one team is dead, that team loses."

"What if a team surrenders?" Eric interrupted.

Druid walked over to Eric and got into his face and lightly said.

"There is no mercy; we'll kill you anyways."

Eric made a gulping sound.

Druid started to talk again.

"With that said, two people will guard each base. The other three will go out into battle. Each game, we'll rotate on who guards the bases. When we get to the bases, we will go over who will guard the first game. Now, without anything more to say, we are going to pick the teams.

Druid named off his teammates.

"Alright, first I'll take Stephen. Then Kevin, John, and Robert." Druid demanded.

They all got up and joined Druid's side.

Martek called his teammates over.

"Jason, Brian, Chris, and Eric."

They got up and joined Martek.

Druid looked at his men.

"Alright everyone, grab your equipment and stand in a line shoulder to shoulder."

His team got all of their stuff together and turned everything on. They configured all of their equipment.

"Testing, this is Commander Druid. Can you hear me?" Druid said in the radio.

"Read you loud and clear Commander Druid." John said.

"Roger that." Robert said.

"Good to go Commander." Kevin said.

"Everything is clear over here." Stephen said.

Druid smiled.

"Excellent. Alright men, this is it, the one battle that we can not lose. Your enemy is tough, but not that tough. We will crush them before they know it. From now on during this battle you will call me Commander Druid. You will be known as the Red Team. Our base is through those trees behind me and onto the left. Commander Martek and his Base will be to the right. Now, if you all are ready, let's go out there and kick some Blue Team ass!"

Everyone raised their guns into the air.

"Yeah…!" The red team shouted.

Druid went up to Martek.

"You guys have twenty minutes to get to your bases. Once that time is up, we're coming for you." Druid said with a dark tone.

"Let's go!" Druid said running into the forest.

The red team ran behind Commander Druid as he led them to the base. They ran into the forest like wild animals, and were only heard as echoes in the dark trees beyond the field. Martek turned toward his team.

"Okay team, you saw how tough they are. We have a fight on our hands but we have something that they don't. That my friends; is a great team. We can beat these guys, and we will. Everyone get your things together. Is everyone ready?"

"We're all good to go Commander Martek." Brian said.

"Excellent team. Testing one two, testing. Can you hear me?" Martek said over the radio.

"Read you loud and clear Commander." Eric said.

"Roger that sir." Jason said.

"Transmission went through fine." Brian said.

"All systems check in over on my end." Chris said.

"Good, we are ready to begin. Are you ready to kick their you know what's?" Martek shouted.

"Let's do it!" The team shouted out.

They all ran into the forest.

Meanwhile back at the red team, they had just arrived at the base ten minutes later.

"Alright team, we are going to have Kevin and Robert stay here and guard the base this first round."

"Roger that Commander Druid." Kevin said climbing the rocks to the top.

"Robert, you are going to guard the bottom of the base and make sure the enemy is killed if they get near. Kevin, from up there you can use your scope to snipe out the enemy from a distance."

"Roger that Commander."

Commander Druid then looked at Stephen and John.

"Alright guys, lets go. We are splitting up. John will take the middle, Stephen will take the West end, and I will have the East end. We are going to head straight that way, but be careful because the enemy is already on their way."

Back at the Blue Team, Commander Martek had already gotten everyone situated in their positions. Chris and Jason were guarding the base. Chris had the lower end and Jason had the higher end.

"Alright Brian, you take the middle, Eric will take the East end, and I will take the West end."

"You got it Commander Martek." Eric said.

"Alright let's go guys. The enemy is near." Martek walked off.

Soon, the teams had all split up.

"Commander Druid, do you read me?" John said.

"I read you. How is everything?"

"All clear on this end."

"Stephen, this is the Commander. Do you copy?"

"I copy sir. Everything here is quiet so far."

"Copy that; so far is the key phrase."

"Roger that Commander."

Just then a little gray squirrel jumped from a tree and right in front of Stephen, which scared him enough to fire his weapon.

"Ah!" Stephen screamed.

The squirrel ran up the nearest tree and was out of sight.

"Stupid squirrel." He said.

Commander Druid heard Stephen and radioed back.

"Stephen, are you okay? Over."

"Roger Commander. It was a stupid squirrel. It scared the living daylights out of me."

Commander Druid and John laughed over the radio.

"Ha ha, very funny you two." Stephen said.

Stephen began walking and all the sudden he saw a red light on his chest. Not long after, he was shot by Commander Martek, and his laser gun automatically shut off.

Commander Druid heard a shot over the radio followed by static, and then nothing. He sat there in silence looking around.

"Stephen, come in Stephen." Commander Druid said.

There was nothing but silence.

"Commander, this is John, I can't get a hold of Stephen anywhere."

"I know John; it looks like we may have lost a man."

"Oh no, who did it?"

"I don't know. Kevin and Robert, do you copy?"

"We read you Commander." Kevin said.

"Stephen went silent. It looks like we lost him."

Kevin looked at Robert in fear.

"Both of you guys be on the look out; the enemy is closer than we thought."

"You got it Commander." Robert said.

"John, be on the lookout." Commander Druid said.

"You got it Commander."

Commander Martek went up to Stephen.

"Looks like you're dead buddy. Just stay here. When the game is over, your laser pack will turn back on and you'll be told to head back to base."

Commander Martek ran past Stephen and into the bushes ahead, running fast toward the Red Base.

Commander Druid on the other hand was furious and wanted to kill himself an enemy. John made his way through the forest without seeing anyone. He arrived at the Blue Base but couldn't see anyone there. He had the idea that he would climb up a tree and scope out the base from up there. John quickly got to the nearest tree, and climbed up to a high enough spot where the entire base was visible. He couldn't see anyone from up there. All the sudden, he saw a head pop up from on top of the base. It was Jason.

"Looks like a sitting duck to me." John said taking aim.

"All clear so far Commander Martek." Chris said.

Chris wasn't in sight. He was on the back side of the base walking around. Jason however, was in plain firing range atop the rock.

John lined up his crosshairs and took aim. When he had a shot, he took it. John pulled back the trigger and fired at Jason. Jason felt his laser pack vibrate and then shut off on him.

"I've been shot!" He said to Chris out loud.

"What? You were shot?"

"Yes." Jason rolled his eyes at Chris.

Meanwhile, Commander Druid was hot on the trail. He could smell the sweat off of a person that wasn't far off.

"Commander Martek, this is Eric. Are you there?"

"Go ahead Eric."

"I am located at the edge of the hill near the hedges. I am knelling down in hiding because I could have sworn I felt someone watching me. So far I've got nothing."

Commander Druid could hear a faint whisper through the trees ahead of him. When he got through the trees, he saw a few hedges that blocked the way down the hill. Commander Druid was also on the East side of the hill.

"Eric, where about are you on the hill?" Commander Martek asked.

"I... Well I don't know. I can see downtown from over here."

Commander Martek knew exactly where he was. The only place you can see downtown Riverdale was at the Far East end of the hill.

"You are at the East end Eric. Lie low, I'll be there in a minute." Commander Martek said.

"Roger that Commander."

Eric sat there waiting, but as soon as he looked up... Total silence. Commander Druid had fired his weapon and killed Eric, shutting off his laser pack.

"See what happens when you camp?" Commander Druid said.

Back at the Blue Base, John was still sniping out the area.

"Alright buddy, where are you at now?" John said scooping out the base.

"Commander Martek, this is Chris. Do you copy?" Chris shouted.

"I copy. What's going on over there?"

"Sir, we have heavy gunfire in this area. The base is under attack. Do you copy?"

"I copy that. I am on my way!" Commander Martek shouted as he ran toward his base.

Commander Druid ran toward the Blue Base to help John take over the area. Commander Martek on the other hand was running as fast as he could through all of the heavy brush, hoping that he could get there in time. Without watching where he was going, all the sudden he tripped on a small rock and tumbled down the ravine at the center of the forest, leaving him with a loud scream all the way down.

Druid stopped blank in his tracks as he heard the loud echo of someone screaming throughout the land.

"Anyone and everyone, do you copy?" Druid said.

John was the first to reply.

"I copy Commander, what is going on?"

"Did anyone hear someone scream just now?"

"Negative. Everything is all quiet over here."

"Stop the game; we have to make sure everyone is accounted for."

"Roger, what's going on? Why are we stopping the game?" John asked.

"I need to make sure everyone is okay. John. Is Chris still at the base?"

"That's affirmative; I was just about to kill him until you ruined my shot."

"Call Chris and tell him the game is over. We need to make sure everyone is okay." Commander Druid ordered.

Stephen got on the radio.

"Hey guys, what's going on? Is the game over?"

"Steve, this is Druid, do me a favor and see if all of your team is around. I heard someone scream nearby and I am going to check out what it was."

"Alright man, be careful." Stephen replied.

Back at the Blue Base, John called the game and shouted for Chris.

"Chris! The game is over. Something is going on and Druid said that he heard someone scream. Can you hear me?"

Chris emerged from the rock formation at the very top of the base.

"What's going on John? What about a scream? Are you joking? Cause if you are I swear ill shoot you down from that tree."

"No dude, I am not joking around. Do me a favor and call everyone on your team and see if they are all okay."

"Chris come in, this is Brian."

"Go ahead man."

"Dude, can you get a hold of Martek? I can't seem to get in contact with him. All I hear is static on his end."

"You got to be kidding me. Where did he go?"

"I don't know but I'll keep trying." Brian said.

Chris ran down the base to meet up with John. John jumped down from the tree and walked toward the base.

Druid was still looking around and could find nothing but a crack the size of a bus in the ground. He looked down inside of the crack and couldn't see the bottom anywhere.

"Druid, this is John."

"Go ahead."

"Chris and I are here at the blue base. As far as everyone is concerned, we are all here minus one."

"What do you mean minus one?"

"It's Martek, he's not responding to our calls."

"None of them?"

"No, not a single one."

Druid looked around him to see if he could see anything. The only thing he could hear was the sound of the forest and the air whistling through the trees.

"Martek!" Druid shouted out in all directions. "Where are you!"

Absolute silence came across the forest. Martek was nowhere to be found.

"Alright guys get everyone together and meet up where we picked our teams at the east side of the forest right now." Druid radioed in.

Everyone responded and quickly went to the rendezvous point.

Back at the meeting spot, everyone was trying to figure out what was going on. They were all there except for Martek. They all knew that Martek was truly missing.

"Okay guys, we need to find Martek right now. Who was the last one to hear from him?" Druid demanded.

"I think it was me dude." Chris said.

"What was the last thing he said?" John asked

eagerly.

"I was under attack and I called Martek for help, and he told me that he was on his way toward the base where I was. After that, that's the last I heard from him."

"Anyone else?" Druid asked.

Everyone shook their head.

"No." They all said.

"Alright, well let me tell you what I heard. I heard someone scream at the top of their lungs somewhere in that forest. I am guessing that it was Martek, but I am hoping it wasn't. We need to figure out what we are going to do because it is getting to be dark out. The sun is going down in about a half hour and our light will be gone."

"Druid, it's no use to go look for him in such a small timeframe. We need to go back and let his Mom know what the hell is going on." Brian demanded.

"I'm up for that." Stephen got up and said.

After a long pause, Druid made up his mind.

"Alright everyone, we'll go back to Martek's house and let Sarah know what is going on. I think it is too much for us to risk more people getting lost or hurt out there anyways. We have to get going right now though. I couldn't imagine what happened to Martek, and I really don't like this at all."

Everyone got up from the ground and headed down the trail to the bottom of the hill. When they got to the bottom of the trail, Druid looked back up at the top and wondered if Martek was okay.

"Come on Druid, he'll be fine." John said dragging Druid back.

CHAPTER 6

It was dusk, and the darkening forest was once again an empty desolate area. Everyone went home... Well almost everyone. Martek was still missing. At the center of the forest below the opening in the ground, was Martek lying on the ground face up. The area he was at was still out in the open. There were still many trees in the area as well as lush and fertile grass. The grass was so green in fact; it was the only area in which grass was that pure in the forest. It was clear that the area was different somehow.

Martek opened his eyes slowly and looked up to see the half moon shinning through the dark blue twilight sky directly above him. It was as if the moon was looking down on him because of it being exactly straight up. The Sun however, was just above the horizon getting ready to set for the day. As he got up, he looked around and could see that he was still in the forest.

"What happened?" He said holding his head looking around.

As he walked around figuring out how to get back home, he stumbled upon a circle of trees not far from where he fell. As he got toward the center of the circle, he noticed a perfect circular green patch of the freshest grass he had ever seen. Around the patch of grass lied a circle of dull quartz crystal rocks that surrounded the grassy area.

"Wow, what is this?" He said in amazement.

After a few minutes of investigating, the sun had finally set. As the moon shinned directly above him, he noticed something coming from the moon. He stood there in awe just looking up. A bluish white beam of light faded in and became visible to Martek's eyes. The beam of light shinned directly on the patch of grass including the rocks that surrounded it. As the light became more intense, the light scattered into hundreds of beams throughout the rocks to form a spider web made of light. After the light was done scattering, the rocks turned into brilliantly crystallized quartz crystals and glowed like the moon. Martek looked in shock and all the sudden; a sword appeared before him that stuck directly in the center of the circle, emitting masses of energy all around it. At the very top of the sword's hilt formed the letter M that glowed bright blue. Martek covered his eyes as the light was so blinding, he couldn't look at it any longer.

At this time, John and Druid were the only ones at Martek's house. Everyone else had to leave back home. They were waiting for Sarah to return home. Sarah had gone out and no one knew where and why. Druid looked behind John and saw up on the hill, an extremely bright beam of light shooting straight up into the sky.

"What the hell is that?" Druid said in shock as he turned John around to look at it.

"Oh My God, what is that?" John said.

"I don't know, but what ever it is, I'm going to check it out."

John and Druid ran down the street toward the Riverdale Hills.

Everyone around the city saw the same thing and stopped in their tracks as well. The cars on the freeways were at a mere stop as people got out looking at the beam of light that came from the hills to the west.

Meanwhile up on the hill, Martek looked at the sword for a few more seconds before making a decision. He stepped up to the circle of light and slowly reached his hand out inside of the beam. He felt nothing that would endanger him, so with slow pace he crossed inside the circle until he was standing in front of the sword that stuck into the ground before him. Hesitant at first, he slowly reached out to the handle of the sword with both hands and gripped onto it tightly. With one easy pull, the sword was free into his hands, and he was engulfed by white energy blocking his vision from outside of the circle.

A few seconds later, the white light faded away until it was completely gone. He looked around and saw that he did have the sword in his hands. As he stepped off of the circle, he noticed that the rocks were still shinning their brilliant color. He looked down at the sword in his right hand and examined its detail from blade to hilt. After carefully examining the sword, he looked up at the moon, which once again was a normal moon that shinned in the night sky.

John and Druid were running up the trail that led to the top of the hill. They noticed that the light was gone and was nowhere to be found.

"The light, it's gone!" Druid yelled.

After they got to the top, Druid called out for Martek.

"Martek!" He screamed out loud.

Druid listened in but still nothing.

Martek was walking in the forest trying to figure

out a way to get back home. Suddenly he heard a ringing in his ear followed by a voice that called his name. He stood there and listened in.

"What in the world is that?" He said. "I swear I am hearing things now."

Martek kept walking along, and this time, he heard it again. Only this voice wasn't the same as the last one.

"John?" He said to himself in amazement.

"John!" He yelled out.

John and Druid heard Martek yell out, and they ran as fast as they could toward the voice. After several hundred feet of running, they finally met up.

"Martek! We found you!" Druid screamed out in joy.

"Hey guys! It's great to see you. You have no idea."

After all of them caught their breath, John looked over to Martek's hand and saw the sword he was holding.

"What is that Martek?" John pointed to the sword.

"This?" Martek said holding up the sword.

"Whoa!" Druid said in amazement.

"I found this sword somewhere back there. I woke up and seriously the sword appeared out of nowhere. Then there were light shows all around, it was so cool. And then the sun, and the moon, and…"

Druid stopped Martek.

"Dude, how hard did you hit your head?" He said.

"This is bogus." John said to *himself.*

"No it's not John." Martek said.

John's eyes turned wide open as he knew it was impossible to hear him, but Martek somehow did.

"Wait a minute, how did you know what I said?" John said demandingly.

"I… I don't know. I just heard you say something, that's all."

"Ok wait a minute, this is freaking me out." Druid said. "You read John's mind?"

"I think I can."

Just then they heard a sound coming from the eastern skies.

"What is it?" John asked.

"Lets get out of here guys, those are helicopters." Druid said.

All of them ran down the hill as fast as they could until they got to the bottom of the hill and through the chain link fence. When they all got to the other side, two helicopters flew past at high speed toward the top of the hill, with their spotlights on.

Druid took off his jacket.

"Here Martek, take this and use it to wrap the sword up."

"Thanks."

Martek took the jacket and wrapped up his sword.

"Come on guys, we should get going back to the house. I don't think I want to be out here much longer." Druid said to both of them.

"I'm with you." John said.

All of them turned toward the street and walked back home still hearing the faint sounds of helicopters.

A half hour later, they all got back to Martek's house. The streets were dark and the air was quiet. You could still hear the faint sounds of the propellers from the helicopters that were still at the Riverdale Hills. They stopped as they got close to Martek's front porch to look back at the hills.

"Looks like they are still investigating." Druid

said looking at the helicopters in the distance.

"Hey Druid, what exactly made these helicopters come in the first place?" Martek asked.

"Well dude, we saw a bright light shoot straight from the top of the hill and into the sky. I swear everyone in this city must have seen it, including law enforcement; and I am betting that they called in military forces to check it out."

"Yeah man, we are not kidding when we say a bright light." John said.

"Well you should have seen it where I was. I was practically blinded by the light."

Martek looked down at the sword in his hands. The sword was still covered by Druid's jacket so no one else could see what Martek had found.

"Come on guys, let's go into the house and be as far away from this as we can." John said.

Everyone walked to Martek's door and went into the house.

Inside the house John and Druid went to the living room and sat down. Martek walked directly passed them.

"Where are you going?" Druid asked Martek.

"I'll be back. I'm going to go and hide this somewhere in my room." He said holding up the covered sword.

Martek went into his room and put the sword on his bed and uncovered it. He looked at it still in utter shock.

"What the heck is going on today?" He said.

He picked up the sword and walked over to the mirror near his closet and looked at himself holding it.

"This is pretty cool." He said.

He pretended that he was in the middle ages fighting in a battle. After swinging it once, he accidentally hit his nightstand lamp and shattered it into hundreds of pieces. The lamp flashed a bright purple before going out.

John and Druid heard the loud crash down the hall.

"Hey are you okay in there?" Druid yelled out.

Martek stood there in the dark.

"I'm okay!" He shouted back.

Martek looked around and thought that he could see faint objects around the room. The objects looked as if he had a white light on, on a very dim glow. The objects started to pulsate in brightness, until he realized that he might be seeing in the dark.

"What the... No this can't be. Impossible."

He rubbed his eyes as hard as he could and counted to ten. When he reached ten he uncovered his eyes and saw nothing but pitch blackness.

"That's better. My eyes must have been playing tricks on me." He said.

He took the sword and felt around the room for his bed mattress, so he could hide the sword underneath it. He found the mattress and hid it. After he hid the sword, he went out to the living room and sat down on the couch and talked with John and Druid.

"Okay, so about how you knew what I said." John said to Martek.

"What about it?"

"How did you know? I mean can you do that for any purpose, or was that just some lucky guess."

"I don't know man. I guess I can do it every time. It's just that ever since I woke up in the forest after falling, I just haven't felt the same and it's not in a bad way at all either."

"Well dude, we are going to see exactly what this is. Don't you worry about this Martek, I am sure it is nothing." Druid said.

"Yeah that's easy for you to say. You haven't been through what I have gone through today, and what I am going through right now. I could swear I could see…" Martek paused.

"See what?" Druid asked.

"Never mind." Martek said looking down.

"Okay… Dude I am going to give you a test and we have to get to the bottom of this whole thing whether it was just a coincidence or not that you read John's mind."

Martek looked over at Druid.

"A test on me… What kind of a test?"

"I'm going to think of a number from one to ten and you are going to guess it."

"That's crazy. There is no way I'll be able to guess what is in your mind man." Martek complained some more.

Just then, Martek saw above Druid's head, faint images of numbers floating around. The numbers appeared to be moving around as if they were caught in a whirlwind. Just then, he heard Druid's voice echo into his ear.

I'm betting that Martek won't guess what number I am thinking of. I really am thinking of the number five but I never said anything about the number zero.

Druid gave a sharp smile, and he saw Martek raise his eyebrow up at him.

"What?" Druid said.

"Oh nothing, I could have sworn you were trying to trick me. I know that zero is a number."

Druid's jaw dropped as if a million pounds was strapped to it.

"How in the hell did you know that dude?" John asked.

Druid still sat there with his jaw hung open, and his eyes as wide as the full moon.

"Hey Druid, are you okay?" Martek asked.

"How… How in the world did you know what I

was thinking about?" Druid asked in shock.

"Look I don't know. I just heard your voice, but your mouth wasn't moving. It was as clear as if it was you talking normally. I heard you say the number five first, and then the number zero."

Druid jumped up out of his seat and stood there.

"You knew that I was thinking of the number five first? Oh my God, now I know that you are serious!"

"Look Druid, calm down okay. It isn't you that's supposed to be freaking out here. I am starting to hear what everyone is thinking and I am trying to block it all right now. I will find a way to channel this somehow but I am seriously freaked out myself so just calm down. It's not like I am going to use this what ever I have; to do anything that will make anyone mad. All I know is, I found something in that forest and ever since I woke up, I seriously haven't been the same. Okay?"

"Alright man, we are with you to the very end. We'll figure this out with you dude." John said.

Druid sat back down.

"Yeah man, hey I am sorry about freaking out but it's just not everyday someone can actually prove to you that your mind can be read. That's a true ability right there man." Druid said.

"Alright it's my turn. I'll think of a number and you guess it. I won't freak out like Druid, so let's do this thing." John said.

"Alright." Martek agreed.

John sat there and started to think of something. Martek on the other hand could clearly see that it was not a number that John had in his mind, but a shape. He saw a cloud form above John's head. The cloud formed into the shape of a triangle. No number was found and no voice could be heard.

"It's not a number John, you are cheating."

"So what dude, let me know what it is. I want to

know for sure."

"It's a triangle." Martek answered back.

"Wow dude, you are right. It was a triangle. It looks like you do have something going on. We are going to keep this on the hush-hush until we figure out what it going on."

"Okay, that is a good idea." Martek said looking down to the floor with a confused look on his face.

Just then, Sarah came home.

"Martek?" She said walking around the corner.

She saw Martek, John, and Druid sitting on the couch.

"Martek. Where did you go? Everyone was looking for you. Is everything alright? What happened?"

"I'm fine Mom, really I am."

"I got a call from Eric's Mom and she told me everything that happened. She said that you were missing and that no one could find you. I am really glad you are home now. You have no idea how scared I was when I found out that no one knew where you were at."

"I am fine Mom, it is okay. I'm home now."

"I'm going to go call Eric's Mom back and let her know that you are back so she can call off the search. The whole Police Department was getting ready to look for you."

She walked into the kitchen and picked up the phone, dialing Eric's Mom's phone.

"Gee Martek, I wish my Mom was like that when I was missing." Druid said.

John looked over at Druid.

"Dude you have never been missing so I don't know why you think your Mom isn't like that."

"Oh yeah, that is true."

They laughed.

All of them listened in on the conversation between the two moms.

"Hi, this is Ms. Majestic. Martek is home right now. He isn't missing anymore."

There was a long pause.

"I know, I know, thank you very much though for your help. I appreciate it. Okay. Will do… uh huh… bye…"

She hung up the phone and walked back into the living room where everyone was.

"Alright, so now that everything is okay I wanted to know if you guys were the ones staying the night tonight."

"Yes, it is us. You know we are your favorite." Druid said smiling.

"Yes, you are." Sarah said shaking her head. "By the way you two; did you call home and let your parents know that you will be spending the night here tonight? I wouldn't want another parent wondering where in the world their kid is at night." She smiled again.

"John and I will do that right now."

John and Druid got up and headed to the phone to call home and tell their parents that they were spending the night at Martek's house tonight. John didn't need to tell his parents because his parents knew about it since last night. Druid just called home to check in and remind his Dad that he and John were staying at Martek's tonight.

"Hey Mom, what exactly are we having for dinner tonight?"

"We're having T-Bone steaks. I know you love them, they are your favorite!"

"That's sweet! Thanks Mom!"

"You're welcome. How about you and your friends find something to do for the next forty minutes or so, and I'll get dinner ready."

"Alright Mom, thanks again!"

Martek got up and walked over to his friends.

"Hey guys, want to go outside and shoot some hoops while dinner is being made?"

"Sounds great to me!" John said.

"What are we having for dinner?" Druid asked.

"My Mom is making T-Bone Steaks. They are the best!"

"No way, I can't wait! I always love your Mom's cooking." Druid said.

"Yeah, my mom is one hell of a cook."

They all went outside to shoot some hoops in the backyard at the basketball court.

Martek walked over to the basketball and picked it up.

"Pass it here!" John yelled to Martek with his hands wide open.

"Here you go!" Martek passed the ball to John.

"Alright, so we are going to play some nice Horse. Does that sound cool?" John said.

"Sounds fine to me." Martek said to John.

"I'm up for a little game of that." Druid added.

They started to play the game and it was Druids turn to shoot. Druid took the ball and shot it at a nice distance but shot too high causing the ball to get stuck in the tree next to the hoop.

"Oh great, that stupid tree took the ball." Druid said.

"It's okay guys; I climb this tree all the time. I'll go get it."

Martek ran up to the trunk of the tree and began to climb it. Up and up he went, until he was about level to the basketball.

The tree was full of leaves in the center, but branches branched out of it in all directions so it was easy to be at any part of the tree and stand on it.

"I see it!" Martek yelled.

Martek walked off of the center part of the tree

and onto a rather thick branch that led to the basketball. He walked outward toward the ball using his hands to hold onto the branch on top of him so he didn't fall. As he got closer to the end, the branch started to crackle. Martek stopped.

"Be careful man." Druid said looking up.

He got directly where the ball was and reached out for it with one hand. He couldn't reach down that far, so he had to reach more and more letting his fingers lose more grip from the branch he was holding onto.

"Almost got it…"

Martek reached too far, and then slipped. He started to fall and he grabbed a hold of the bottom branch and hung there with his hands right next to the ball.

"Martek, hold on! I'm coming up!" Druid said running up to the tree trunk.

"I can't hold on much longer dude. I'm slipping!"

Martek hung there for a few seconds and lost his grip and fell from the tree.

"No!" John yelled out has he covered his eyes.

All the sudden, silence came over the air and not a sound was to be heard; not even the wind.

"Guys." Martek said.

John and Druid uncovered their eyes and saw the unthinkable.

They looked up at Martek, and saw him with his arms outward floating directly below the ball.

"What in the…" John said in shock.

Martek looked from side to side.

"Am I?" Martek said.

"Yeah… Yeah I think you are." Druid said confused.

Martek looked at the ball just in front of him and reached his hands out toward it. He glided in mid air toward the ball until it was in his hands. He looked at the ball and nodded his head.

"What's happening to me?"

"I don't know, you might want to come down though before someone else sees you." Druid said

Martek turned his head and that made his body turn around. He looked down at John, and then at Druid, who was half way up the tree looking at him. Then, he dropped the ball and thought really hard to just go back onto his feet and stand. He started to float down slowly until his feet touched the ground.

Martek stood there looking down at the ground with a very puzzled look on his face.

John and Druid walked up to him.

"Hey, are you okay?" Druid asked.

"I thought I was a goner man. I thought I was going to die right here. I don't know what's going on today, but I honestly can say I am not use to it. I mean, I don't even know what to do with all of this?"

"Look dude, what ever this gift is I am sure it is for a reason. You told us what you found. You told us what it did to you, and you made a believer out of both of us. If I were you, I wouldn't worry about this, and I would just figure out what this is. I promise after dinner we are going to find out what is going on and to tell you the truth; I'd give anything to do what you just did right now up there. How did it feel?" Druid said.

"You know what man. It felt like nothing I have ever felt before. My stomach was in my head. My whole body felt like just one thing and I couldn't feel my feet. I could only feel my arms and it was just weird. I don't know if I will ever do that again, or if I can. It might have been just a one time thing."

"You think so?" Druid said smiling.

Druid gave Martek the ball.

"Now make that ten foot slam dunk. I know you can do it."

John smiled.

Martek turned around to face the net. He took one deep breath and took off running toward the hoop. With both hands around the ball, Martek made his final step and leaped up into the air passing up the hoop and up into the sky higher and higher.

"Whoa!" Martek screamed as he was going up over the roof of the house.

Martek couldn't control his movements in the air so it was hard to do anything while stuck up there. Martek waved his hands around like he was out of control, and started to fall back to the ground this time over the house. He fell and hit the front lawn and rolled onto the street and lay there.

"Oh man." Druid said.

John and Druid rushed around the house to see if Martek was okay.

"Martek! Are you okay?"

They saw him lying on the ground on his back breathing and laughing.

"Why are you laughing? I thought you hurt yourself." John said.

"Far from it John, far from it." Martek said as he got up.

Martek had absolutely no scratches on him although his shirt that he wore was completely torn up.

"You are lucky dude." Druid said.

Just then, Sarah opened the front door.

"Guys, what are you doing out here?"

"Oh hi Mom, we were playing Basketball and the ball went over the roof and into the front yard. Don't worry though, everything is fine."

"Okay good. Dinner is ready. Come inside and wash up and let's get grubbing."

They all walked inside and headed to the bathroom to wash up.

After everyone was seated at the dinner table, they

began to dig in.

"So how was your birthday?" Sarah asked.

"Mom, the day was great. Thank you so much! Everything was cool, including the part where I got lost."

"Well I am glad you all had fun. You know the only thing that got me worried about you was the fact that there were helicopters, and a story is brewing up at the news station about what happened over in the Riverdale Hills tonight."

"Oh you mean that light that was in the sky, and then when Martek..." Druid covered John's mouth and smiled at Sarah.

"What he means is, that the light we saw, and we thought Martek was in serious trouble and we were worried and went up to get him." Druid quickly said.

"Oh... Well yes it is a relief that you guys found him."

"Yeah, I am glad they found me. Today has just been weird is all, but this dinner is great Mom, thank you!"

"Yeah it is great." John and Druid said.

"Thank you boys."

They sat there and ate for several more minutes and just talked about random stuff.

"So... What does the news say of the light that was seen up in the hills?" Martek asked in hope to find out any more information.

"Nothing right now actually, they say it could be a prank, but other sources are trying to say it is aliens and what not. It is a crazy story and I doubt anyone will find anything. In fact, when I was a kid the only thing I saw up there that was really neat was just a circle of trees and a fire pit. I am not sure what happened to that place, but a bunch of friends and I loved to go up there at nights and have a bonfire and tell scary ghost stories."

Martek knew exactly what she was talking about.

Of course it was no bonfire. There were a circle of rocks but no burned areas. He thought maybe she might be talking about something else, but then again it would make sense why the circle was never thought of as sacred. The circle itself was merely disguised as some sort of a bonfire pit, but was really hidden deep inside to be some sort of gateway or portal.

Dinner was over and Sarah cleaned up the table, while everyone else went to Martek's room to hang out.

"Hey dude, what do we do now?" John said to everyone.

"Let's do what I said we were going to do after dinner." Druid replied.

"And that is?" Martek added.

"We are going to figure out what the heck happened to you Martek."

"Alright man. How do we do that?"

Druid walked over to Martek's computer and logged onto the internet.

"Simple guys, we are going to see if anything like this, or similar to this has happened before."

"I see. What exactly are you looking for?"

"Martek, get your sword out." Druid said.

Martek went to his bed and picked up his mattress to reveal the powerful sword. He took the sword and showed it to Druid. Druid took the sword from Martek, and examined it. The blade was completely clean with not a trace of dirt, grime, spots, cracks, or anything. The sword was pure and solid on each sides of the blade going from the tip to the hilt. The hilt was clearly solid gold and silver, with a decorative crown on the very top. There were no letters or ancient scripture on the sword, so it was extremely hard to pick out where it came from. The sword was clearly seen to be some sort of a medieval piece; however it looked far from a traditional medieval sword. It actually looked more like a wizard's sword, than a knight's sword.

"Hmm… This is very interesting guys. I haven't seen anything like it in my life. This sword is seriously nothing I have ever seen." Druid said as he examined the sword.

"What do you think it is dude?" John asked.

"I don't know. Maybe we can search something on the internet."

Druid got onto a search engine and typed in a few things.

"Okay, let's try Power Sword."

When the search was over he found little on power swords. The only thing that came up the most was the sword Excalibur.

"Okay guys, we have Excalibur. There isn't anything else here. It says a mystical sword known as Excalibur was pulled from a stone by a boy named Arthur. This was about thirteen-hundred years ago somewhere in the country of Wales. It says that Arthur became one of the greatest kings to ever live, and he had a powerful wizard Merlin to help him do what was right and never wrong. It says Merlin was also like a Father to Arthur, in which he raised young Arthur into the only man to take the sword."

"Okay, like that tells me a lot. If this sword were Excalibur, then I will win the lottery today." Martek said.

"Dude, it's a sword that has some sort of magic in it, right?" John stood up and said.

"Yeah."

"Well Excalibur had the same thing, right?"

"Right."

"Then why shouldn't it be Excalibur?"

"Hold on a second guys. There is a photo drawing of what Excalibur was said to have looked like."

Druid clicked on the link and the picture downloaded. All of them looked at the drawing.

"This sword looks nothing like the one I have in my hand guys."

"I have to agree Druid. Martek's sword is way different. If you look at the hilt of the sword, they aren't even the same design or shape. The blade on this sword looks a lot the same. If you look at the shape of the sword, Excalibur looks more like a Roman Sword with a short hilt, and Martek's sword looks more medieval with the wings coming out of the handle."

"Yeah man, you are right. This can't be Martek's sword." Druid closed the window.

"So guys, what do we do now?" Martek said confused.

Druid stood up and walked around the room thinking. After about ten seconds of pacing, he had an idea. He went up to Martek, and sat him down on the chair.

"What if you had more abilities than you already do now? Think about it." Druid said to him.

"What is there to think about?" Martek answered.

"You can be the very first real superhero on the face of this planet. Think about it man. We can have a costume for you and everything. I am seriously thinking about this. You can already fly, you can read minds, and you have super hearing. I bet you can do so much more."

"Like what?"

"Like night vision, x-ray vision, maybe walk through objects, and super speed."

"Okay, how do you expect to test these powers out?" Martek asked.

"Well first I just want to see more of what you already do know, except for flying, cause I don't want you to hit your head on the ceiling or go through the roof. That's all you need right now is a big hole in the ceiling in your room."

They all laughed.

"Yeah you are right. I actually want to see if the sword has any powers at all."

"That's a good idea Druid, I am curious about the sword."

"Okay, let's see what the sword does."

Martek gripped the sword in his hand and held the blade up toward the ceiling, with the hilt near his chest. He closed his eyes and concentrated really hard at what he went through when he found the sword. He thought of the moon, the energy, and the light that came from it. Suddenly the blade of the sword began to glow a bluish white color.

"Are you seeing this dude?" John asked Druid in shock.

"I'm seeing it." Druid said while hypnotized to Martek's sword.

Then, a beam of light shot from the sword and into the ceiling. Air can be felt coming from the sword, going in all directions radiating out from it. Just then, Martek's hands began to glow as well. The glow and energy moved up from his hands and throughout his entire body until it completely covered him. He opened his eyes and smiled. Then the energy subsided and faded away.

"What happened?" John asked eagerly.

"Guys, I don't know what happened but I just felt like I got the biggest charge of my life. I still feel the energy going through my veins."

"Strange. I bet your main power is linked to the energy somehow." Druid said.

"What do you mean?" John asked.

"I mean Martek has the power to do anything with energy. He can manipulate it, use it, and do anything. I'm willing to bet on it. If that's true, you will have the best abilities any superhero has ever had. Martek, I want you to try something, and think of energy and think really hard at what you want to do, and try that out."

"Okay."

Martek took his hand and pointed it toward the wall on the right of him and concentrated really hard. After a few seconds of waiting, a beam of light shot from his hand and into the wall. The computer lamp in his room started to flicker.

"I knew it. He does have the power of energy." Druid said proudly.

Martek put his hand down, and the energy faded away. He looked at his hand and smiled.

"You were right Druid. It is energy."

Druid walked over to Martek.

"Yeah buddy, it is."

"Okay enough of this, how about some ice cream guys?" Martek said.

"Let's do it." John said walking toward the door.

"Wait a minute." Druid stopped them.

"What?" Martek asked.

"We forgot one thing."

"And that is?"

"Didn't you mention something about seeing something, and then you said never mind?"

"Oh... that. Yeah I did."

"What was it?"

"Well... Remember that loud crash you heard in my room when I was putting the sword away?"

"Yeah." Druid said.

"Yeah, well that was actually me breaking the nightstand lamp. You notice I only have my computer lamp on." Martek answered back to him.

"Okay."

"When the nightstand lamp broke, it was pitch-black in my room. Then after a while, I started to see shapes and things."

Druid smiled.

"What was it?" John asked Druid.

"I know exactly what he is referring to and if you have what I think you have; then this is one hell of ability."

Druid walked over to the computer desk and reached for the lamp. Just then the room became completely dark.

"What's going on?" John asked.

"Hey Martek." Druid whispered.

"Yeah?"

"What do you see?"

Martek looked and he saw the same shapes again, but this time he could tell they were outlined as people. There were two figures in front of him, and after several seconds, he could clearly see that it was John and Druid.

"Guys, I can see you. The light isn't even on though. Everything around is gray and has no color."

"That's because you have a case of night vision." Druid said.

"Night vision, are you serious?" Martek asked.

"Well you can see in the dark, can you?"

"Yeah I can. John, if you put that finger up again, I will break it."

John put his hands in his pockets and looked as if he didn't do anything.

"Man that is not fair. You could see what I was doing."

Druid went over and searched for the lamp switch to turn on the light. After a few seconds, he found the switch and the light came on. He looked back at Martek and John smiling and shaking his head.

"That was awesome. Okay guys; now let's go get some ice cream." Martek said.

They all walked out of the room and down the hall to get some ice cream.

"Hey Martek, what flavors are there?" John

asked.

"We have tons. We have chocolate, vanilla, mint, and all kinds."

"I'll take the mint." John said.

"I'll go ahead and take chocolate."

"Awesome, I am taking chocolate too." Martek finished.

They all got their ice creams into their bowls and went to the dining room table to eat. When they were all seated, Martek noticed that he forgot something.

"Oh man! I forgot my ice cream." Martek said.

They all laughed.

"Where is it?" Druid asked.

"It's over there." Martek said pointing to it on the countertop.

When Martek pointed at it, something amazing happened. The bowl lifted up from the countertop and started to float toward him.

"Are you doing that?" John asked.

"Of course he is dude, who else would be?" Druid said as he stuffed a spoonful of ice cream into his mouth.

Martek concentrated hard as the bowl floated toward him. His hand went from pointing at the bowl, to reaching out for it, getting ready to catch it. The bowl floated closer and closer, and then right into his hand. Martek looked at it, holding it in utter shock.

"Well, I think Martek has what we call Telekinesis." Druid said proudly.

"What's that?" John asked.

Martek took the bowl and set it in front of him, taking a bite of his ice cream.

"Telekinesis is when someone uses their brain to move objects from any distance without touching them."

"Oh okay. Well that explains it." John laughed.

"Yeah guys. I think I am done with this whole

magic stuff for one night. Let's go ahead and do something like play a nice game of Counter-Struck." Martek said.

"I'm up for that man." Druid said jumping up.

They all got their ice creams and headed to Martek's room to play a game of Counter-Struck.

An hour later, they were done with the game and decided to do an important thing.

"Hey Martek, remember talking about Superhero stuff?" Druid asked.

"Yeah... What about it?"

"Well, you know what we should do now is figure out the design of a possible costume in case you decide to do that."

"That's a good idea." John said.

"Yeah, perhaps it is a good idea. I'll get the pencils and paper out of my desk, and we'll figure it out."

Martek walked over to his desk drawer and took out a pencil and a sketch pad. He walked back over and they all started to think.

"Okay, well first of all, we have to figure out what you want to be called." Druid said.

"How about Black Boy?" John said.

"Why on Earth would you say that?"

"I don't know you guys. I figured since Martek likes that color, maybe we should call him something like it."

"No, that is nowhere near good enough. However, you did give me an idea for his main color John."

"What's that?"

"Hey Martek, I just figured out the perfect main color for your costume." Druid said excitedly.

"What is it?" Martek asked.

"Black."

"Black, don't you think that's a little dark?"

"Well… Not all black. We can make different colors too. What other colors do you suggest?"

"Well, since my sword and energy seems to be revolving around the color blue, we should go with blue."

"That's a good idea, I like it." Druid said.

Druid wrote down all of the information.

"Hey, on your sword, what is that letter I saw on the top of the hilt?" John said.

"I don't know, let me go get it."

Martek went and pulled his sword out, and looked at the top of the hilt.

"You're right; there is a distinct letter on this sword. It is the letter M."

"I am thinking strongly on making your name revolve around that letter. We will use this letter in the sketch of your costume." Druid said.

Druid began to sketch out the outer part of the figure.

"Okay, so the suit itself is going to be black so we'll make it black. You mentioned something about blue so where do you think the blue should go?"

"Well, I think my boots and gloves should be blue."

"You want gloves?" Druid asked.

"Well since I have a sword, I think gloves are appropriate."

"Okay, so you mean gauntlets?" John stepped in and said.

"No; nothing like that. I am thinking on the lines of thin leather gloves. You know the flexible kind."

"Okay so we have so far the black suit, blue gloves, and blue boots. I personally think since you fly, you need a cape."

"That is actually a good idea." John said.

"Yeah, that is huh."

"Okay so now we have the cape. Should we make

it black?"

"Yes. Well, wait. No."

"No?"

"I am thinking on like two colors. Have the blue in the inner part of the cape and the black on the outer part. What do you think?"

"I actually like that idea." Druid said sketching it in.

"How about a utility belt," John said.

"No, actually that isn't a good idea. He doesn't need a utility belt. What he can have is a belt; perhaps a blue belt?" Druid said.

"No, actually lets make the belt a silver colored belt." Martek corrected.

"Silver, why silver?" Druid asked.

"Because my sword has gold on it and silver, this will lead me to the next addition to the costume."

"And that is?" Druid asked.

"Every hero has a symbol on their chest, back of the cape, and the center of the belt buckle. I want this symbol to be a dark color, and I think I have just the symbol."

Martek took a sheet of paper and began to sketch out the symbol. After a minute, he was finished and showed John and Druid.

"Looks like an M." John said.

"Exactly, the letter matches my sword."

"Good idea. But that would mean you hero name would have to start with that same letter." Druid said.

"We'll think on the name later. A dark symbol like this is going to be on my chest. I don't want anything on the back of the cape. The actual letter will be somehow inside of my belt buckle, which the buckle will be a dark gold color."

"Okay, I got it." Druid said drawing out everything.

When Druid was finished with the drawing, he showed Martek and John.

"Is this okay?"

"Perfect! It looks great man! Great job!"

"Thanks Martek. John, do you like it?"

"It's actually a costume and I could see this being made. But it's missing one thing."

"What's that?" Martek asked.

"A scabbard hooked onto his belt on his left side."

"Oh of course! How could I be so blind?" Druid said.

"What's a scabbard guys?" Martek asked.

"A scabbard is a holding where you can put a sword. It is generally hooked on the belt of the person for easy access to take the sword out and put it away."

"Oh I get it now. That is a good idea!"

Druid drew the scabbard onto the drawing and made it black to match his costume.

"There you go Martek, we are all finished. Now all we have to do is get the stuff to make this costume, and figure out a name for you."

"Great job. Thank you so much. It looks great."

"No problem, I am tired so I am going to hit the hay."

"Me too." John said.

"No problem guys, I am going to sleep too. I had a long day, we all have." Martek said.

Everyone got ready to go to sleep and they all slept soundly into the night.

CHAPTER 7

While Martek was sleeping peacefully, something was disturbing him in his dream. It was the same dream that he had the other night. He violently shook out of his dream, wiping the sweat from his forehead.

"Hey, are you okay?" Druid whispered.

"Yeah, I think so. Is John awake?"

"No, he is out cold."

"Okay."

"Well… Goodnight Martek."

"Night Druid."

Druid rolled over, and within seconds fell into a deep sleep. Martek on the other hand got out of bed and reached under his bed to see if the sword was still there. He pulled out the sword and looked at it.

"I guess yesterday wasn't a dream." He said to himself.

Martek, still in his clothes looked outside of his window and walked out of his room. He made his way down the hall very carefully so he wouldn't wake anyone up.

Martek sat outside atop his roof at the corner of the house just above his mom's room, looking up into the sky just thinking. It was twilight out, only the brightest of the stars could be seen. Some moderately bright stars were still visible. The air was a pleasant warm feeling. It wasn't a cold night at all. Martek looked up at the sky and began to speak softly to himself.

"Why me? What is it about me that should deserve anything like this? Yesterday was amazing and it is almost too good to be true. I don't even know who I am anymore. I mean, I knew who I was, but now; no way."

Martek looked toward the brighter horizon; it would be dawn in less than an hour. He looked down at his sword and nodded his head smiling. He stood up and took another chance. He took a giant leap straight up into the sky. As he climbed higher into the sky, the air got cooler and crisper. He felt the changes of temperature by the different altitudes. A low flying cumulus cloud was coming straight from above him. When he went through it, he was expecting a fluffy feeling. Instead of the fluffy feeling, he was splashed by water in his face. He wiped off the cool water from his face and kept going up. Still not used to the feeling of flying, he took some time practicing. He flew up toward the sky and back down. He learned to stop but it was more of a glide for him. He tried and tried until he got the hang of stopping. The secret to flying he found out was that all you had to do was to think what you wanted to do, and which direction you wanted to go, and it would happen. Of course this wasn't going to happen for everyone, but it did for him.

"You know, this is a lot like learning how to ride a bike. A lot of it is more mental than physical." He said.

After getting used to some of the flying, he tried to twist while flying; and to turn and do loops. He did a fairly good job at some of the maneuvers. Now it was time to see what the sword could do. He took the sword in both hands and held it out toward the sky above him, and gathered all of his energy in his body directing it toward the sword. The sword glowed bright blue, and shot out a burst of energy into the sky.

"Wow that was pretty cool."

After a while he thought of something obvious. Why his hat never seems to come off of his head? He knew that at the speed he was flying, and how much the air hit him the hat would blow right off; but it didn't. He reached up and tried to pull his hat off of his head, it was stuck.

"What the heck? Why can't this thing come off?"

He pulled and pulled, but it was no use. The hat was just not coming off. It was molded to his head.

"I wonder if this is only like this while up in the sky."

He decided to head back home. The sun was out at the altitude that he was at, but dark on the surface below him. He looked down to see if he could locate where he was. He saw downtown Riverdale to the south of him and knew that his house was still below him. He noticed the small park next to his house and found it finally. He glided back down toward his home, taking caution so he was not to be seen. When he got just above his house, he slowly went down to the roof. The neighbor's lights out in the backyard was on, so he knew they were awake. He could hear the shower running in his neighbor's bathroom. When he landed on the roof it wasn't a very soft landing, but soft enough.

He was right above his Mom's room and he didn't know if she heard him or not. He leapt down from his roof and went back inside. After he went to his room, he slowly got into his bed and lied down.

Druid woke up.

"Martek, why are you still up?" He whispered.

"I was practicing a few things."

"Oh okay."

"Hey I have an idea. Remember when you mentioned about being a Superhero?"

"Yes."

"I think I'm going to use my birthday money on making a costume. I am going to take that idea and go for it. I was given these powers for a reason; I should put them to good use."

"That's good to hear man. Should we go to the mall today and go to this really cool place I know of to buy stuff for your costume?"

"Yeah which store is it?"

"It's a new store that just opened. It is called Custom Apparel. You can get anything there from belts to spandex. I think you are going to need some Spandex, since that seems to be the best thing for a costume when it comes to a superhero."

"Sounds great, I'm going to get a few more hours, and I'll see you when I wake up."

"Yeah good idea, I'm still tired. Night!"

"Night man."

Both of them fell into a deep sleep once again.

It was nine o'clock when Martek's alarm went off. Everyone jumped up and got ready for the day.

"Why is everyone so excited?" John asked them both.

"Because today we are going to the mall my friend." Druid said.

"The mall, why are we going there?"

"Martek is going to get himself some things to make a costume."

"Are you serious?"

"Yeah, I figured I need to do something if I have these crazy abilities."

"That's really cool. I am glad. Are you going to that new store that just opened? What was that name again..." John thought on the name.

"Custom Apparel." Martek answered.

"Yes that's the one. Okay good, because it is next door to my favorite place."

"What's that?" Martek asked.

"From the Earth. It's a place where they have real gems, rocks, and minerals. I am a gemologist freak!"

"Oh okay."

"Rise and shine everyone! Last one to the table is a rotten egg!" A voice yelled from down the hall.

"They all finished getting ready and bolted down the hallway to the dining room table. When they got there, they saw stacks of pancakes and bacon.

"Yum!" John said sitting down at the table.

"Morning boys." Martek's Mom said.

"Good morning!" They all said.

"Breakfast looks great mom, thank you."

They all sat down and ate.

"Hey Mom, do you think you can take all of us to the mall today after breakfast?"

"I don't see why not. Anything particular you are looking to buy?"

"Maybe, but Druid wants to show me this cool place that just opened; something about Halloween costumes and such."

"Sounds fun, I'll take you guys when we are done with breakfast. Druid, you can eat as much as you want since you are a growing boy." She laughed.

"Thanks Mom." Martek said.

"You're welcome Hun."

Just then his Mom looked at Martek in shock. She saw something that she could swear was there before.

"Martek. Where did that bruise go on your arm?"

"What bruise?"

"Hello? The bruise you got when you fell in the bathroom on Friday."

Martek looked at his arm where the bruise was, and it was gone.

"Oh wow, I don't know. I guess I'm a fast healer."

"I have never seen anyone heal that quickly before."

"I have seen it; there was this crazy thing on the TV the other day and yeah."

"Well okay. You forgot I work for the news station didn't you? She smiled.

After a while of eating, they all finished up and cleaned up the table. When everyone was done, they got all of their stuff ready and went to the car and waited for Martek's Mom.

Martek's Mom met them all in the garage, and she unlocked the car doors. They all got in and buckled up. Martek was of course ridding shotgun. When everyone was set to go, Martek's Mom started up the car, and opened up the automatic garage door. The car backed out of the driveway, and headed down the street and off to the mall.

"Alright, so what are you going to do when you get there John?" Martek turned and asked.

"I'm headed to that new rock shop that they have. I don't know about you, but I got to check that store out."

"Yeah while you do that, Martek and I will be at the store next to you gathering some stuff."

"There's a new rock shop John?" Martek's Mom interrupted.

"Oh yes, I heard it is suppose to be the best. You can see anything in there that has to do with the Earth, and her minerals. There are Diamonds, Emeralds, and all kinds of gems. You can also see a bunch of other things like volcanic rocks and such. The best part of it is all that stuff you can buy; if you had the money."

"Wow, you can buy the diamonds too?" She asked eagerly.

"Yes, you can buy anything."

"That's really neat, maybe Martek and I will check it out after we gather our stuff in the other shop." Druid said.

"What exactly are you getting Druid?" Martek's Mom asked.

A long pause came over the car. Just then Druid was saved from telling her anything by the sound of the radio.

"Oh wait hold on." She said turning up the radio.

This is a KRCT Special Report. A Severe outbreak is being closely monitored for the Riverdale county section Tuesday night possibly bringing in heavy rain and severe thunderstorms. Latest weather analysis has shown the possibility of a Tornado in these dangerous events. Although events like these are extremely rare in this section of the state, the National Weather Service advises to take all necessary precautions as this is a Potentially Dangerous Situation. Teamed up with the National Weather Service is the Ontario Weather Service, where Meteorologists Kevin Martin and Joshua Young are saying this is indeed a big one. We had an interview with Kevin and Josh and they said that they will not rule out the possibility of a tornado in this system, although many news stations and weather stations have downgraded this system to just thundershowers. The big question on everyone's mind is. Will this storm be as strong as earlier predicted? Only time will tell. The storm is expected to make landfall from the beaches and move inland on Tuesday Evening and last a good portion of the night. This is Brandon Baxter reporting in, stay tuned for updates.

She turned down the volume of the radio and

everyone sat in complete silence.

"Okay so what the heck was that all about?" John said.

"Didn't you hear? They are saying that some big storm is headed our way." Druid added.

"That's pretty intense Mom. Do you think they are right?"

"I don't know. The Ontario Weather Service has been extremely accurate on storms like these for a while now, and hearing that they are forecasting a bad storm gives me the creeps."

"Yeah I know Mom, but it's a nice day today."

"Uh dude, Tuesday is three whole days away. You might want to wait and see." John said.

Martek sat there thinking. He didn't have to wait and see; he already could feel something coming over the horizon. He stopped thinking about it to block his thoughts.

"Let's all listen to some music." Martek's Mom said switching to a rock radio station.

All of them listened to the music, and slowly forgot about the weather.

They arrived at the mall and she pulled the car on the side of the curb at the front entrance. They all got out of the car.

"Okay boys, it's just about half past ten. I want you guys to be out here at three."

"Okay Mom, thanks!"

They all walked to the front of the mall as Martek's Mom drove off. They entered the mall and looked around. It was Sunday, so there were a lot of people at the mall. They walked to the directory and looked at the map. John immediately found 'From the Earth', which was located right above the food court on the second floor.

"Hey guys, I found it!" John said pointing at the

map.

"Yeah, you did alright. It looks like it is right above the food court. We are lucky they are next door to each other." Druid said.

"Tell me about it. Hey since it's up on the second floor, I'll meet you guys up there." Martek said smiling

"What do you mean?" John asked.

"Martek's being a smart ass." Druid said shaking his head and smiling.

"What did I do? All I said was…"

"You said nothing. John, you, and I will be taking the elevator like normal shoppers. Understand?"

"Awe man, where is the fun in that." Martek smiled.

"By the way dude, you couldn't do that anyways. Do you know how many people would see you?"

"True…"

They all walked from the map and to the elevator just across the way, which would take them to the second floor. On their way up, Martek had some humor of his own.

"This is boring." Martek said.

"Why's that dude?" Druid asked.

"Because, this thing goes up so slow." Martek grinned.

"Enough of that; not everyone has what you have."

"Yeah, I would kill to have what you have." John said.

They reached the top, and got out of the elevator. There, in front of them in all its glory, was their destination.

"We made it!" John said running toward the store.

"We'll be next door! Don't mind us!" Druid yelled at John. But John was too excited, he ignored

Druid completely.

Martek and Druid saw the store Custom Apparel and went in. There, they saw tons of costumes and accessories. There were full made costumes, and there were half made costumes. At the end of the store, they saw the different colors of fabrics and designs, which were seen in many options. There was brick pattern, zigzag, striped, poke a dot, checkered, plain, etc. There was everything, including every color you could ever think of.

"Wow, this place is awesome!" Martek said.

"Yeah it is."

They went to the back of the store and looked at all the different types and colors of fabric.

"Okay, for a basic costume we will need some spandex."

"Good idea, let's get the dark grey."

Druid picked up the dark grey spandex, and took several layers. He also took some blue spandex for the cape, even the black kind for the emblem.

"Price isn't that bad." Druid said.

"I know, this place rocks! Hey, check that out." Martek said as he pointed toward belts and belt buckles. They both walked over to see all the different kinds of varieties.

"Wow dude, look at all of these belts and buckles! You can make anything here. They have cowboy belts, space belts, regular belts, leather belts, and so much more!"

Martek looked over every belt, and just about in the center of the selection was one belt that didn't match any of the rest at all.

"What is this?"

He took out the belt and looked at it. The belt was a silver belt that resembled a space warrior belt, with an oval dark golden buckle attached to it that looked in great condition.

"I want this one man, its perfect!"

"Yeah, I'll say. It's like this thing was made for you dude."

Martek took the belt and held onto it, looking at it in amazement and awe.

"Okay so we have your spandex and belt... What else is on the list?" Druid asked as he took out the paper, which contained the costume information.

"Okay, we have the gloves and the boots left. That is over there in that section, and it looks like we are done after that."

They both walked over to the boot section and found everything from cowboy boots to space boots.

"Okay we have red hero boots, blue, and black. I think you wanted blue, so we will get a pair of these leather boots. What size do you wear Martek?"

"Size twelve."

"Okay, same as me. So are these okay? Try them on."

"Try them on?"

"Yes dude, try those on."

"Okay..."

Martek sat down at the bench behind him and put on the boots. They fit very snug on him, and he liked how he could move around in them.

"How do they fit?"

"They fit great man!"

Martek looked at them in the mirror in front of them, and liked them so much that he didn't want to take them off.

"Okay buddy, back in the box they go."

"Oh okay." Martek said sadly.

He took off the boots and put them back in the box.

"This matches your blue spandex perfectly, man."

"Yeah I know that's why I like them too."

"Okay the gloves are over there; let's see what kind they have." Druid pointed.

"No need, I already see the ones I want."

Martek walked fast to the glove section and grabbed the blue pair of thin leather gloves, and matched them up with the boots. The colors were perfectly matched, and the texture of the gloves matched as well.

"Perfect, looks like we have a match." Druid said.

"Yeah we do!" Martek said smiling happily.

Just then, while Martek was looking at Druid, his smile went lower and lower. Druid noticed something was wrong.

"What's wrong man?" He asked.

Martek stood there in silence as if he saw a ghost.

Druid noticed that Martek was looking a little over his right shoulder, he moved out of the way to see what it was. He saw nothing but a wall of merchandise.

"Okay man, what is going on? Are you okay?"

"Dude, do you see that man?"

"See what? A wall, gloves, what?"

Druid tried to figure out what it was but couldn't. Martek on the other hand, was witnessing a robbery in the store next to the one they were at.

"Hey, can you hold onto my stuff? Here's the money to pay for it, I'll be right back."

He threw the stuff into Druid's hands, and slipped him the cash. Within seconds, Martek was already out of the store.

At From the Earth, a robbery was in session. There was only one robber in the store, and he was armed; pointing his gun in all directions.

"Alright everyone, listen up! This is a hold up. I want all of you to stay where you are; don't even move."

The robber took out a money bag from his jacket

pocket and threw it in the cashier's face.

"Alright, I want you to fill it right now!" He screamed.

The cashier shook violently as the robber pointed the gun at his face, but complied with the robber's demands. As the cashier started to fill the bag with the money and jewels, Martek came into the store. The robber looked over at Martek and started to scream at him.

"Get on the floor! Get down or I'll shoot!"

Martek stood there with his fists clenched.

"Are you deaf? I said get on the floor before I put a bullet in your head." The robber said in anger.

The robber was now so agitated he walked up to Martek in quick pace and put the gun to his forehead, and Martek felt the barrel of the gun on his skin. Without hesitation, he took the robber's wrist that held the gun, and grabbed it away from his forehead. Martek took the gun out of the robbers hand and threw it behind him toward the entrance. The robber swung a hard right at Martek, but he dodged the punch. Several times the robber swung at him, but Martek could see his every move before anything came close to him. John was watching from a short distance, and immediately noticed that Martek was moving faster than anything he had ever seen. Everyone who was watching was amazed. After several seconds, Martek was tired of the robber and grew angry. He took the robbers hands as they came close and broke both of his wrists. He grabbed the robber by his shirt and threw him into the front entrance wall about ten feet away. Everyone gasped. The robber started to get up, and he noticed the gun on the floor in front of him.

"Everyone stay back." Martek said looking behind him.

"Martek, look out!" John yelled.

Martek looked back to the robber, who had his

gun pointed in his direction. Without any time to waste, a shot was fired at Martek. Martek flew back and fell on his back as the robber fled out the front entrance. Everyone started to crowd over Martek.

"Martek!" John yelled running toward him.

It was clear to everyone that Martek was shot, as they could see a bullet hole in is shirt on his chest. Immediately the store clerk called for help.

The cashier and all the employee's started to shove people away from Martek.

"Alright everyone, give the boy some air!" They shouted.

Everyone backed away from Martek; all but John.

"Martek, please speak to me. Martek, can you hear me?" John said with tears in his eyes.

Druid walked into the store and saw Martek on the ground, and ran toward him.

"What the heck happened? Martek! Can you hear me?" Druid said as he knelt down.

Just then, Martek started to move his head from left to right slowly at first, then his eyes opened and he looked around him.

"What happened guys?"

"You were shot. Are you okay?"

"I think so."

Martek started to get up, but the cashier told him to stay down.

"No you have to stay where you are; you have been shot for heaven's sake. An ambulance is already on its way."

Martek looked down at his shirt and put his finger in the bullet hole, and felt a smashed coin like object against his skin. He pulled out the object and everyone gasped in shock and disbelief.

"Is that…" John said.

"That's the bullet." Druid replied with eyes wide

open.

"Are you bleeding?" John asked.

Martek took his shirt and lifted it up to see if he was bleeding, and there was not one mark on him.

"That's impossible; we all saw you get shot!" The cashier said.

Martek got up to his feet, and stood there looking at the bullet in his hand that was smashed from the impact. A smile came over him.

A Police officer came into the store and walked toward the cashier.

"Is this your stuff in the bag?" The officer said.

"Yes it is, thank you sir." The cashier said taking the bag from the officer.

The Officer turned to the crowd and looked around.

"I want to speak to the one who stopped the robbery." He said.

Martek stood there and raised his hand.

"I did." He said.

"Will you come outside with me? I have to ask you a few questions."

"Sure."

Martek and the police officer walked out of the store. Martek saw the robber across the way face down on the ground in handcuffs.

"First, I will ask for your name." The officer said.

"Martek."

"Do you have a last name?"

"Yeah, it's Majestic."

"Sounds familiar; okay so what went on in there?"

"Well officer, that man was robbing the store. I came in the door and he told me to get on the floor."

"And why didn't you?"

"He didn't give me enough time. Then he pointed the gun at me and I was in shock. He started screaming at me, and then he walked up to me and put the gun on my forehead."

"After that… What happened?"

"After that, I guess I attacked him and defended myself so I wouldn't get shot…"

"Okay and he said he shot you. Did you get shot? What is that hole on your shirt?"

"Oh, I don't know if he shot me. I mean, I am not bleeding and I have no mark on me. The hole looks like a bullet hole but I'm not sure."

"I see. Okay that's about it. We are taking this guy downtown and he's going to face quite a bit of time in prison."

"That's good news."

"Thanks for the assistance, we'll see you around."

The officer walked away from Martek, and joined the rest of his men. John and Druid walked up to Martek to see how everything was going.

"So what did he tell you?" John asked.

"He told me that they are taking the guy to jail."

"That's obvious." Druid laughed.

"Hey man, I have a question. How in the heck are you still alive?" John asked.

Martek smiled and pulled the smashed bullet out of his pocket.

"This is why guys."

John and Druid looked at the bullet and smiled. They knew exactly what Martek had, and what had happened.

"Wait a minute, I get it now! This explains why your bruise was gone this morning. You heal so fast. Not only that, but this bullet is proof that you might even be invincible." Druid said.

"Invincible?" Martek said.

"Yeah, this is one super ability that all real superheroes need to have."

"Okay, well I didn't feel a thing if that's what you are going to ask next; just small pressure."

"What time is it?" John asked.

Druid took out his cell phone and checked the time.

"It's about noon right now."

"Thanks Druid. Do you guys want to head back home? I have the stuff in the bag. Can I use your phone to call my mom?"

"Yeah, let's go home man." Druid said giving Martek the phone.

Martek dialed home and asked his Mom to pick them up from the mall.

"Okay, yeah… Thanks Mom."

Martek gave the phone back to Druid.

"Thanks, she said she is coming over right now. Let's go out to the front and wait."

They all walked to the front of the mall and waited for Martek's Mom to pick them up. They sat on the front planters at the front of the mall. Martek turned to Druid and John.

"Hey guys, are you going to come back to my house and stay to make the costume?"

"Yeah man, you know we are going to help you!" Druid said.

"For sure we will be there." John added.

"By the way Martek, we have to sew this thing. Do you know how you are going to do that?" Druid asked.

"Yeah I do. Remember the sewing class I took in freshman year?"

"Yeah."

"I still remember how to do it, and my Mom has a sewing machine too."

"Sounds like a plan to me, that's a relief on the sewing."

Minutes later, Martek's Mom pulled into the driveway of the mall parking lot and picked them up.

They got into the car.

"Hey Mom, thanks for picking us up at such short notice."

"You're welcome. What happened here? I heard something on the news, and I see tons of police around here."

"There was a robbery at a store."

"I know that, they said a teenager was involved. Do you know who it was?"

Martek, John, and Druid looked at each other and paused.

"Any of you guys know?" A longer pause.

They didn't want to lie to her, so they just didn't say anything.

"I'm sure I'll find out on the news, but this would make one heck of a story. Some reported that this guy was shot, but nothing happened. They didn't get his name, and the police refused to leak out any information."

They all went back to Martek's house.

At Martek's house, they got into his room and took out everything in the bag and set it on the computer desk. They switched all of the lights on; what was left of them any ways.

"Okay guys, I'll be right back. I have to go get the sewing machine from my Mom."

Martek walked out of the room and went to get the sewing machine from his Mom. He went down to the kitchen where his Mom was at making some sandwiches for lunch.

"Hey Mom, can I borrow the sewing machine for a school project I am doing?"

"A project, what kind is it?"

"It's a renaissance project for school. Its extra credit and I figured it would be something fun to do."

"Oh of course you can, the sewing machine is in the hall closet on the top shelf."

"Thanks mom!"

"You're welcome. Here, take these sandwiches with you so everyone can eat some lunch. And here are a couple of drinks to go with it."

She handed him the food, and Martek smiled and walked down the hall into his room.

"Lunch time guys!" Martek said.

"Alright!" They both shouted.

"I'll be right back; I have to go get the sewing machine."

Martek walked out of the room and opened the hall closet door. He looked up and pulled out the sewing machine. He walked back to his room and placed it on the computer desk. After that he joined his friends and they ate their lunch.

After a half hour, lunch was over and they started to get to work on the costume. Just then, Druid's phone started to ring. He answered his phone.

"Hello? Oh hey Mom... Yeah... Six? No problem, I'll see you then. Thanks Mom... Okay, bye." He hung up the phone.

"What'd she want?" John asked.

"I have to go home at six. She is picking me up, so I have a couple hours."

"Okay. Hey can I use your phone to call my Mom?"

"Sure."

John called his Mom, but unlike Druid, he had to go home right away. His Parents were leaving the house for most of the day, and he had to stay at home with his little brothers and sisters to watch over them.

"Bad news guys... My Mom's coming to pick me up right now. I have to baby-sit the little brats."

"Oh that sucks." Martek said.

"Yeah that does." Druid added.

"Oh well; thanks for coming to my birthday party and hanging out, it has been something."

"You're welcome. Yeah it really has huh."

They got started on the costume. Martek went to the desk drawer and pulled out the drawing of the costume. He plugged in the sewing machine and they started with the main color fabric.

"Okay. Dark grey is going first."

"Hey Martek, have you figured out a name for you yet?" John asked.

"Nah, I was thinking on flyboy."

"What the heck kind of name is that?"

"I was only kidding. I'd rather be caught dead with that name."

They continue working on the costume with the main piece of the suit. Everything that was dark grey on the costume was sewed together. He sewed the arm pieces together and made the bottom part of the costume. After doing so, he started on the cape. He wanted the cape to be as far down, as the middle of his calves. The cape consisted of black on the outside and blue on the inside, but the blue will be after everything black was applied. Soon after, the cape was done, they looked at it. They found that it looked better as an all blue cape, so they made it all blue

"Okay, I did the cape, something is missing though." Martek questioned

"What is it?" John asked.

"I want this cape to have some sort of string, so I can tie it under the arms and have it flow out of the costume."

"I see what you are talking about. Why don't you just sew some strings made of spandex onto the cape? Like put one string on the left and the other on the right. How is that?" Druid said.

"That's a great idea man, I'll do that."

"That's awesome man. What on the suit is going to be blue?" John asked.

"I believe the drawing has it. The entire cape is going to be the blue gabardine. Also the tights are going to be blue as well." Martek explained.

"You're wearing tights? You mean underwear worn inside out?" John chuckled.

"It's not underwear John, a whole bunch of other superheroes in the comics has been seen in the same thing."

"Yes, I am going to be wearing tights." He said looking around.

A voice was heard from out in the hall.

"John! Your Mom just pulled in!" Martek's Mom said.

"See you later guys. Thanks for the party Martek, it's been real."

"Thanks for coming dude, we'll see you later."

"Later John."

John got his things together and walked out of the room shutting the door behind him.

Martek and Druid continued on the costume.

"Alright, the cape is done." Martek said as he held it up.

"Looks great, man."

"Thanks. The suit is done as well, I need to go ahead and do the details on it. The chest area will have the logo M on it."

Martek flipped through his sketch pad and found the symbol page.

"Okay, we have several symbols, but this is the best one I think."

He showed Druid the symbol, and he agreed as well.

"Yeah, that is the best I think. How are you going

to do the emblem?"

"The black is perfect for the emblem. It's going to blend in nicely with the dark grey."

"I agree dude."

Martek got the black spandex, and started to draw the outline carefully. He got the scissors, and started cutting out the outline. When the cutting was complete, he looked at it and smiled.

"This is definitely it man." Druid said proudly.

"I agree."

Martek spread the suit onto the table, and started to sew it on to where the symbol was on the drawing. The symbol was sewn in after several short minutes. When it was finished, he looked at it and made sure it was centered between the chest creases.

"Perfect. Can you hand me the cape?"

Druid reached for the cape and handed it to Martek. He looked at his cape and thought that the cape was very nice indeed.

"This cape looks awesome!" Martek said.

"Sure does."

"I'm not going to put a blue M on the back of this cape, I've decided. What do you think?"

"That actually makes sense then."

Martek took the cape and draped it over the bed behind his computer desk, and gathered a few other things for the next task.

"Alright, we are not done yet. We have to make the scabbard for the sword, and sew it onto the belt."

"Right, let me go get the leather out of the bag."

Druid got up and headed to the closet where he had tossed the bag of materials. Just as he was about to get the bag, he saw a baseball and picked it up. He turned around and faced Martek.

"Hey Martek; think fast!"

Druid under-handed the ball to Martek. He

missed the catch, and the ball was headed straight for the window. Martek turned around as quick as he could, determined to catch the ball, but something shocked him. He looked at his window and he saw the ball just inches away from it, floating in the air as if someone had just stopped it in mid air. He looked back over at Druid, and he stood there wide eyed looking at the ball. Like the ball, Druid was also frozen stiff. Martek got up and walked over to Druid, and brushed his hand in front of his eyes, but not a breath, sound, or motion came from him. Martek walked over to the ball and looked at it. He looked extremely close and noticed that the ball was moving, but incredibly slow. He reached out to the ball and grabbed it.

"What the heck!" A voice yelled from behind Martek.

Martek turned around, it was Druid.

"Did you just…"

"Just what?"

"I swore that ball was going to break your window, and now not even a split second later, I see you standing there with the ball in your hand." Druid said rubbing his eyes.

Martek looked in shock and then at the ball in his hands. He got up and slowly walked over to Druid.

"You're not going to believe this; I think I may have been moving at super speeds."

"Super speeds, how do you figure? I mean, I believe you since you got the freaking ball in your hand."

"I don't know how I did it. I just turned around and looked at the ball floating in front of my window, and then I looked at you and you were frozen stiff. I even walked to you and brushed my hand in front of your eyes, and you didn't even acknowledge the fact I was there. I walked to the ball, and I could have sworn I could see it moving extremely slow toward my window. I reached out and grabbed the ball, and I heard your voice. It's almost as if..."

"Time stopped for a spilt second." Druid said.

"Yeah, it's like I slowed down time enough to do what I needed to do."

"I'm glad it didn't hit your window, but man you have super speed!"

"I know, I know. This is getting weirder and weirder ever day."

They got back to work on the costume and after putting together the scabbard and the belt, Martek knew something was missing.

"Hey Druid, do you think my belt buckle needs an M on it too?"

"That couldn't hurt."

"I know. How am I going to do that?"

They sat there for minutes thinking, and suddenly Martek had an idea.

"Dude I got it! Wait right here."

Martek got up and went to his closet and looked for something he needed. He found it and showed it to Druid.

"An un-lit candle, wow..." Druid had a puzzled look on his face.

"Not just a candle, watch."

Martek set the candle on top of his desk and looked at it without blinking. He concentrated at it as much as he could.

"What's supposed to happen?"

"Hold on, let me concentrate."

Martek continued to put all of his concentration on the wick of the candle. Martek noticed that a blue halo of light started to circle his vision. He continued to look at the wick, which by this time started to smoke. Tiny blurs of white smoke was seen coming from the top of the candle. He stared at the candle and Druid saw a thin blue line of energy come from his eyes and within seconds, the top of the candle burst with a small flame, and the candle was lit. The halo faded away, and Martek picked up the candle and smiled.

"What the heck was that dude?"

"I knew I could somehow use this energy in a different way. I think I created a beam of energy so hot, it lit this candle."

"That's amazing! Did it hurt?"

"No, I saw a blue circle of light around my vision, but felt nothing but a warm sensation in the inner part of my eye."

"Wow that is really cool man. What are you going to use that for?"

"I had this idea that maybe I could imprint the M into the front of the belt buckle with the same method I used for the candle."

"That's actually not a bad idea. You know cutting through metal is going to take something hotter than what you just did right."

"Yes, I know that, and that is why I'm going to make the beam hotter."

"Alright, don't hurt yourself."

"Hurt myself? You forgot I was shot in the chest right?"

They both laughed.

Martek set the belt buckle onto the top of the desk, and looked directly down on it. He concentrated so much that his eyes began to glow a bright white, until a beam of light pierced the buckle. The buckle started to shake a bit, and Martek held it tight on the table. He began to concentrate on the direction of the beam as he began to carve the letter M into the front of the buckle. When Martek was finished, he picked the belt up and looked at it. Druid started to laugh.

"Oh my God dude. I don't think that worked at

all too well."

Martek held the belt buckle in front of his eye and could see right through it, and Druid was laughing so hard he almost fell off of his chair. The letter didn't even look close to an M, more like a smudge.

"What's so funny?"

"Dude... Look at your desk."

He looked at his desk and he noticed that he had pierced his desk as well. He looked at his floor and immediately noticed that he had also shot straight into the ground.

"Oh great, I wonder how far I shot into the stupid ground."

Druid just sat there laughing, trying to keep up with his breath.

"I don't know man, but that is seriously funny!"

Martek started to laugh too.

"Yeah, I guess it's pretty funny huh."

He took the belt and set it on the desk.

"I guess I will have to watch out how hot my energy gets."

"Dude, it's not called Energy. What you have is called Laser Vision. You'll call it Lasers."

"Okay, whatever fine... Laser Vision." Martek smirked.

When both of them were calm, it was now over and the costume was complete. The scabbard was attached to the belt, which was adjustable to Martek's waist. The suit was finished, and the cape was completed. The boots were already the right color so it was time to try it on.

"Hey Druid, we are done. Do me a favor and watch for the door so My Mom doesn't see this; and turn around and don't face me while I get changed."

"With pleasure, dude." Druid laughed.

Druid got up still laughing, and stood watch at the

door. He was still laughing a bit under his breath, now wiping the tears from his face. Martek got into his suit. He put on everything he could. The boots and the gloves; and after that he put on the belt. He reached under his bed, and pulled out the sword and placed it into the scabbard, which was carefully measured at the time of making it. The sword fit perfectly. For the cape, he had to put the cape on first, and then slip into the top part of the suit. The cape was strapped under his arms, and he had to pull the cape up though the opening where his head went though. The cape came out and draped behind him. The bottom of the cape was right where he wanted it.

"Are you done yet?" Druid asked.

"Almost, give me a few more seconds."

Martek was now finished with putting on his new costume.

"Okay, I'm done. What do you think now?"

Druid turned around and looked at him.

"Wow, dude that is a nice costume. Sure would win a lot of Halloween costume contests I am sure."

"So you're saying it sucks?"

"No it really is awesome; I have never seen anything like it. I really think it is awesome."

"Thanks!"

Martek walked over to the mirror on the outside of his door and looked at himself.

"I'm lacking the muscles though, but I have some definition."

"I just thought of something… What about your super strength? Has it changed?"

"I don't have that. When I lifted up the mattress to get my sword I didn't feel a difference at all. The mattress was still a bit heavy."

"That really sucks man."

"It's okay. Other than that, I think I have pretty

much a good base on my powers. Don't you think?"

"Hey, I think it's incredible what you can do, but there is still something missing about you…"

"What is it?"

Druid looked at Martek and smiled big. He walked over to the sketch pad and drew in a black backwards hat on him. He showed Martek, and then walked over and grabbed the hat off Martek's bed and gave it to him. Martek looked at it and put the hat on backwards. The hat then squeezed onto his head comfortably, and was as if it was glued on.

"Of course Druid, I remember this! The hat did do something weird when I put it on earlier today!"

"Dude I think this gives your character a nice touch. In fact, it might help you figure out a name."

Martek looked at himself and he looked at everything on his costume. He noticed his symbol as an M, and the sword had an M on it and everything was based on that very letter. Still unaware what that letter meant, he came out with the official name.

"Martek!"

"Come again?"

"My name is Martek."

"Uh… Yeah it's been that way your whole life."

"No, no, no… Martek is going to be the name of my superhero."

"Don't you think that's kind of obvious?"

"Yes and no. Not many people have this name as a permanent first name. If my name leaked out, not many people other than the ones at school would know who I am. Plus, have you noticed my costume is without a mask?"

"You know what, that makes a lot of sense. I think that's perfect."

Druid put his arm over Martek's shoulder.

"Martek…" Druid said again.

Moments later, a voice was heard outside of the door.

"Druid! Time to go!"

"Wow, its time for me to go already? Is it really six?"

"Wow, yeah it is." Martek said looking at his clock

"Okay man, well I'll talk to you later. I'll see you either online or at school tomorrow."

Druid got his things and rushed out of the door quickly, closing the door behind him. Martek on the other hand continued to look in the mirror. He then noticed something strange and unusual. He stood to the side and noticed that he was growing excess fat on his chest.

"What the heck?"

After looking, he decided that it was nothing. He then practiced taking his sword out from the scabbard and putting it back in. He did so several times, until he got used to it. He practiced his sword fighting skills and the power of the sword. He practiced for what seemed like hours. He took a few fencing classes back in the day so he knew how to handle a sword.

"Martek, dinner is ready Hun."

"Okay Mom, I am changing right now and I'll be out in a minute."

Martek quickly got out of his costume and packed it in a cardboard box. He tossed the box into the closet on the shelf, and got into his regular clothes, and went out to the dining room table for dinner.

Some time after, Martek was done with his dinner and he went back to his room and practiced some more on his powers. He thought about the flying part, and wanted to control inside flight. He looked at his feet and concentrated really hard. Suddenly his feet left the floor until they were about two feet off of the ground. He practiced on hovering there, and just staying still in the air. This maneuver was important, and he seemed to get the hang of it rather quickly. He then went to his closet and put on his costume. After he put on his costume, he grabbed his sword and placed it in the scabbard. He then floated back up and panned left to right gliding around the room. This felt like he was in the pool just floating around, but this was no pool, it was the air. Martek felt that the air was thicker than ever before, but he liked it. After hours of practicing, he put everything away and got ready for bed. It was school tomorrow, and he remembered what Rod said to him. Something was on the horizon and he could feel it. He went down in his bed and fell asleep.

CHAPTER 8

Morning approached and Martek was awakened by his alarm. He reached for his alarm, and smacked the top of it in a frustrated gesture, which broke into many pieces. Martek jumped up.

"What the heck was that?" He said as he looked at his broken alarm. "Great, I broke it."

He got his stuff ready for the shower, and walked out of his room and into the bathroom. He turned on the shower and went to the mirror to clean his face. He screamed when he saw himself in the mirror. He had grown nearly four times his original size, now bigger than Druid. In fact, looking at him, he was bigger than Rod Burns himself. He looked at himself in the mirror, and raised his arm up and flexed it. He couldn't believe his eyes.

"What? This isn't my body! Where'd it go?"

Then there was a knock on the door.

"Martek... Are you okay?"

"I'm fine Mom, nothing to worry about. Thanks for asking."

"Alright, I'm just making sure. Did you fall in the shower again?"

"No Mom, I'm fine. Thanks."

Martek looked at himself and shook his head.

"Here we go." He smiled.

He knew that he had everything a superhero had. He was very happy, yet still concerned why and how his life changed this much. He got into the shower and showered himself good.

After the shower he put the towel around him and slowly opened the door. He looked down the hall and noticed no one was around. He quickly ran into his room and shut the door. After looking for what to wear, he came to the conclusion that nothing was going to fit him as he was way bigger than he used to be. All in one day, it was amazing to see he gained over two hundred pounds. He looked through his clothes, and found a long sleeve shirt that was extremely baggy on him before. He put it on and then grabbed a loose hooded jacket. He looked in the mirror.

"There we go. That seems to do the trick."

He grabbed his things and rushed to his door to open it, hitting his head on a model airplane that hung on his ceiling six feet high. He ran down the hallway and past his Mom, running out of the door.

"Martek, aren't you going to eat some…? Wonder why he was in such a hurry?" She said.

He got to the bus stop where Eric was waiting for him.

"Hey Martek. What's up?"

"Hey Eric, nothing much I guess. I have been having one wild weekend let me tell you."

"Yeah man, you had us all scared for a minute, but I am glad that you are okay."

"Thanks."

"Where did you go?" Eric asked.

"I just tripped in the forest and stuff that's all."

"Oh okay. I see you didn't get hurt so that's a good thing. Did you hear about the shooting at the mall yesterday? My parents told me about it and I asked who it was, and they said they aren't authorized to mention any names. Darn, huh?"

"Yeah, I heard about it, must have been crazy."

The bus came down the street to pick them up at the bus stop.

"By the way Martek, you look different today. I don't know what it is. Did you get a hair cut?"

"No. Hey Eric, I'll meet up with you at school. I need to do something right now and I have some things to think about."

"Okay... I knew something wasn't right. What do you want me to tell the bus driver?" Eric asked.

"Nothing, he won't see me. I'll talk to you in a little bit."

Martek ran from the bus stop out of the buses sight. Eric got on the bus and sat at the window facing where Martek had run off to. He looked at Martek, who was still running in the distance. Martek ran around the corner of a brick wall, and a faint blue streak was seen shooting off into the sky.

"What was that?" He said to himself.

Up in the sky, Martek was flying around thinking of what was going on. So much has happened in the past two days and he needed to know what was going on. If this was healthy for him, or if something bigger was on the horizon. Martek wondered how he could have gained so much mass in such a short time. He could feel the blood going though his veins, fueling up every muscle in his body.

After several minutes he looked down and saw his

school, which was directly below him. He knew it was
time to land, but didn't want anyone to see him. He
located the football field and remembered that on
Monday mornings, no one was out on the field. He knew
this was a good place to land. With swift moves he
slowly glided down to the field and looked around him.
No one was around and he made a quick but soft landing
on the football field. He looked around to see if he was
seen, and couldn't see anyone. He walked from the
football field, and made his way to the front where he met
John and Druid.

"Hey guys!" Martek shouted.

"Hey Martek, good to see you." John said.

"Hey, yeah how is it going?" Druid asked.

"I need to talk to you, Druid." Martek said.

"Okay."

Martek grabbed Druid by the arm and pulled him
aside.

"Whoa dude, watch who you are grabbing; that
hurt!"

"I'm sorry man."

"Geez, since when did you get such a grip."

"That's what I wanted to tell you."

"Wait a minute… No way. You did? You got
super strength?"

"That's not all, grip my arm."

Druid gripped Martek's arm and immediately
knew by its size, something was going on.

"Oh wow dude, you're bigger than me."

"That's not it."

"Martek stopped with his slouch and stood
straight up."

"Oh… My… God. You're freaking taller than
me too?"

Druid was about to have a nervous breakdown.

"Calm down man, I never expect my powers

would transform my body entirely. I thought maybe a lightshow or something but never this."

"You know what this means." Druid said.

"No… What?"

"You are now the biggest guy in the school. Hell, you are the biggest guy I've ever seen in person. Dude, wear my jacket for now because your sweat shirt isn't helping."

Druid took off his jacket and gave it to Martek.

"Thanks." Martek said putting on the jacket.

The bell rang to go to class and Martek headed for P.E.

When he got into the locker room, he hesitated on getting changed because everyone would see him for sure. He decided to write a fake letter and forge his Mom's signature to excuse him from his class. After writing the letter, he put it into his jacket pocket and went to his locker to put his backpack in it.

"Let's go Martek; we don't want to be late again." Eric said walking passed him.

Martek followed Eric out of the locker room and onto the blacktop where role call was always being made. Everyone looked at Martek and wondered why he was wearing a jacket when it was nearly eighty degrees outside. They walked past the football players who were sitting on the bench by the football field talking amongst themselves. Rod was sitting on the other end staring Martek and Eric down like a piece of steak. Martek was aware of the rumors that were going around school of Rod fighting him at lunch. The teacher came out, and Martek walked over to her and gave her the note to be excused.

"You're excused Martek. I hope your arm feels better." Mrs. Wells said as she finished reading the note.

"Thank you." Martek said walking back to his number.

When role call was done, the class walked over to the tennis courts. Martek sat on the edge of the tennis courts facing away from the football practice. Suddenly, a football hit him in the head. Martek looked back at the laughing players, and saw the football in front of him. He looked down at the football.

"Oh yeah, how do you like this?" He said as he walked up to the football.

He picked up the football and crushed it into his hands until all of the air was out of it. All of the players were shocked now.

"I don't see you laughing now!" Martek said as he tossed the flat ball back to them.

"Oh what the hell!" One of the players yelled out.

"Sorry coach." Martek yelled out.

The coach shook his head in shock and disbelief.

"Don't worry everybody; I'll be back in a few minutes. I am going to get another football." The coach said.

The coach ran to the locker room, while the players stared at Martek and couldn't believe what he had done to their football.

"Do you guys want the next football crushed too?" Martek pointed at the players. "If you want to keep your precious little football, I suggest you keep it off my head." Martek said angrily

"Enough of this, I'm going to rip you in half buddy!" Rod said as he walked to Martek.

Just then, the coach grabbed Rod and pulled him away.

"Get a hold of yourself Rod. Do you want to be kicked off the team?"

"No coach, I don't."

"Then ignore him. You guys shouldn't be throwing the football at him in the first place."

"Right coach."

Everyone continued on their practice, and Rod shook out of his attitude and concentrated on the game. Martek turned back around and sat back down on the grass. Eric ran up to Martek.

"Dude, that was crazy. Why in the heck did you do that? And how did you crush that football like that, it takes a lot to do that." Eric said.

"They hit me in the head with a football."

"Oh okay. I better get back to the game."

Eric ran off to continue his game, while Martek sat there thinking.

At lunch, the whole group was eating at their spot. John, Druid, Eric, and everyone was there. There was in fact, one person missing.

"Hey, where is Martek at?" Eric asked.

"I don't know; that's a good question." Druid said.

"Maybe he is still in a lunch line." John answered.

"That's a possibility huh. Hey guys, did you hear what happened today in P.E. between Martek and the football players?"

"No, what happened?" Druid asked.

"One of the guys threw a football at him and he got so mad he crushed the football into a tiny rag and threw it back at them. Rod was so mad he was about to kick Martek's ass, but was stopped by the coach."

"Kick his ass huh? I doubt it." Druid said.

"What are you talking about dude? Rod is twice Martek's size." Eric said.

John and Druid couldn't mention anything, they just kept quiet.

Seconds later, Rod and his friends were walking in their direction.

"Oh great, what the heck is going on now." Druid

said.

Rod walked up to the group and shoved everybody out of the way and got into Eric's face.

"Alright buddy, you and I aren't finished yet. I'm gonna give you something you'll never forget."

Rod pulled back his fist and got ready to swing at Eric. Eric covered his face in fright. Just then, Rod felt something grab a hold of his hand, swinging him around and pushing him against the wall.

"Martek calm down!" Druid yelled out.

Rod struggled to get out of Martek's grip as he looked deep into his eyes. Martek could see the fright come right out of Rod. Everyone around watching the fight was completely shocked as Martek made a fool out of Rod. Martek's jacket was off and he only wore a long sleeved shirt, which was ripped in many places. They could all see he was many times bigger than Rod, and couldn't believe it. Veins pulsed around Martek's muscles. With one hand, he grabbed a hold of Rod's collar and lifted him up against the wall.

"If you ever pick on another person, let alone my friends again, I'll make sure you never recover. Do you understand that...? ...Shrimp?"

Rod hung there completely helpless, but agreed to Martek's demands.

"Okay... Okay." Rod said frightfully

"Now tell Eric you are sorry, and to everyone watching I want you to say you are sorry for anyone you have ever beat up in your life."

"Come on man." Rod pleaded.

"Do it now!" Martek yelled as he pressed Rod against the wall further.

"Okay, okay. I'm sorry for what I did everyone. I'm sorry for beating you up."

"Good. Don't let me catch you picking on anyone else again."

Martek let go of his grip, and let Rod drop to the floor. He turned around and walked down the steps. Just then, Rod got so angry he got up and rushed toward Martek. Within seconds, Martek turned around and swung at him so hard that he flew into the wall fifteen feet behind him, breaking the side of the wooden building. Rod laid there and was helped up by his friends.

Just then, Deputy Hampton made his way through the crowd and ran toward Martek.

"Hey Martek, stop right there!"

Martek looked to see him running toward him and ran away. The Deputy chased Martek down the side of the locker room. Martek turned the corner to the right, as the deputy soon followed after. The only thing that he saw was the empty blacktop, Martek was gone. A brush of wind came across the deputy, followed by a loud crash of thunder. John and Druid had an idea what had happened, but everyone else wondered what that sound was. It was however a very clear day out, so no room for any thunder.

Martek was flying higher and higher, and saw the school deputy get smaller and smaller until he was too small to be seen. He headed toward the direction of his house. Martek saw the small park down the street from his house and decided to land at it. He slowly glided down but saw a woman and her dog at the park. He went around a large tree, so none of them saw him, and landed in the tree full of leaves. He stepped down a bit and glanced over at the woman and the dog. The dog started barking violently as he saw Martek up in the tree. The lady looked over.

"There's nothing there Spot. Come on, it's time for you to go home." She said yanking on the dog's leach.

The woman and the dog walked down the street

and went out of sight. Martek glided down to the ground and walked toward the middle of the park. Suddenly, a voice was heard into the sky.

"Martek." The voice said.

"Who's there?"

Martek recognized the voice but couldn't remember where he heard it from.

"I've come for the sword, Martek."

"Who are you?"

Martek looked around him in all directions and couldn't seem to figure out where the voice was coming from.

"Who are you? Show yourself now!" Martek screamed.

A yellow electric cloud formed in the middle of the park, just in front of Martek. The cloud thickened until a dark silhouette emerged from it. When the cloud faded away, Martek saw the figure in full view. The figure had a black armored suit on, a weird shaped head, and bright yellow eyes. In a distinct way, he recognized the figure.

"Wait a minute. I know who you are." Martek said.

"Do you now."

"Yes, you are the guy I saw in my dream. What were you doing in my dream?"

"I am, but that is not who I am. My name is Solaro, I am known to be the God of the Sun and fire."

A god, huh? What is it that you want?"

"I've come for the sword. Hand it over and I will leave in peace."

"What do you want the sword for?"

"I've watched what it has done to you. You can't handle its true power and I must have that sword now."

"Why do you want the sword so much? And what is this sword any ways?"

154

"It's far too powerful for you to understand."

"Try me."

"Very well; the sword is the sword of Lunaro, a powerful God. Lunaro is the God of the Moon and Light. I am the God of the Sun and Fire. We were close allies at one point but tensions between us became extremely difficult. When we learned about the powers of the swords, I tried to gain all of the power, but it ended up in a battle to the death. By seeing me standing here, you can see who won that battle. Before I could get my hands on the sword, Lunaro had cast it into the Realm of Power, and said only one who truly can handle the power will rip it from the Realm of Power's grip and continue the legacy of Lunaro. I searched all my time for it, and for thousands of years the sword was nowhere. Then, you decided to be the one Lunaro has waited all this time for, and now I am this close to total power! I need one more sword and with the two, I can combine them to make me the most powerful being that will ever descend on the face of this pathetic universe!"

"There are two swords?"

Solaro raised his hand into the sky and a golden staff appeared before his eyes.

"Do not waste my time, I need that sword now."

"I'm not going to give you the sword. You are going to have to get through me first!"

Solaro grew angry.

"Very well."

Solaro raised his staff up into the air, and electricity from all around struck it. The staff began to glow bright yellow, and it shot toward Martek. The blast knocked Martek into the tree trunk behind him. Martek now dizzy slowly got up, not believing what had just happened to him.

"I'm going to give you one more chance to give me the sword, or I am going to kill you and get it myself."

"You can't have it!" Martek said lying down looking up at Solaro.

"Foolish boy, you think you stand any chance against me? I am the most powerful being in this universe, so I suggest you give me what is rightfully mine!"

"If the sword was rightfully yours, why would you let it go?"

"Enough boy, give me the sword now! Or, I'll make sure no one ever sees you again! You won't even exist!"

"No!"

Martek got up to his feet and raised his hand up into the sky, concentrating as hard as he could. Suddenly the sword appeared in his hand.

"You want this sword Solaro? Come get it!"

Solaro shot a solid energy ball at Martek, but he blocked it from hitting him. In return, Martek raised the sword into the sky, gathering up all of the energy around him. He pointed the sword at Solaro, and shot a beam of energy at him. Solaro ducked; dodging the beam. Solaro threw ball after ball at Martek, and the last one hit him but not to the ground. Martek put the sword in both of his hands and gathered so much energy the sword glowed bright white. He shot the energy at Solaro, knocking him to the ground. Solaro got back up.

"You haven't seen the last of me, Martek. I'll be back!" Solaro said angrily.

The yellow energy cloud appeared again, and engulfed Solaro. Within seconds, Solaro faded into the air and was gone. Martek stood there trying to catch his breath.

"Okay what just happened?" He said to himself.

Martek looked around him to see if anyone saw anything but saw that no one was around. He was lucky no one saw him. He looked up into the sky and flew up heading back to his house. He landed in his tree in the backyard and climbed down it; running into the house. He saw that no one was home so he left the sword close by. He grabbed a snack and switched on the television. On the news he saw a Special Report.

"This is Tim Nolen from Channel Seven. Here in Downtown Riverdale, a fire had broken out in an apartment complex just east of Main Street. The apartment complex is being evacuated right now; so far no one has been injured. Paramedics and Fire Crews are on the scene right now battling out this monster fury. We have reports that there are still residents inside the apartment, but none are in the path of the flames. Wait, wait a minute. Okay folks we have some news. A firefighter is stuck in the burning building and no one can locate him. Firefighters are rushing frantically to find him but so far nothing is turning up. They are afraid he is stuck and no one is hearing the calls from his fellow men."

Martek looked down at the sword in his lap and knew what he had to do. He rushed down the hall and into his room. He took out his costume and quickly got into it.

"There must be a faster way to get into this costume." He said as he put it on.

He put the sword in the scabbard and buckled everything up. When he was ready, he ran up into the attic and blasted out of the window toward downtown Riverdale.

Flying faster and faster, Martek raced through the skies, only looking like a blue streak in the sky. He saw the smoke coming from the distant buildings ahead, and then the flames.

"This is it!" He said smiling.

Back at the apartment, flames burst out engulfing

firefighters inside. Many firefighters did escape, but a few were left in the fiery building. After all of the firefighters got out, the chief ordered everyone to stay out of the building.

"Alright men, let's get this fire put out!" The chief said.

The building exploded into larger flames.

"We must have hit a gas line!" One of the firemen screamed out.

"Chief, we have to go back in there!"

"Why? What's going on?"

"Chief, there's still one more man in there! He's one of ours!"

"Oh dear God..." The chief ran out of ideas.

"I'm going in after him!" One of the men said.

The chief grabbed him and pulled him away.

"Those flames are dangerous, you'll be killed!"

The firefighter looked over the chief's shoulder and could see a bright blue object coming in fast.

"Chief, what is that?" He said.

The chief turned around.

"What is that?" He asked in shock.

Like a missile, the bright blue object was headed straight for them. Everyone thought it was a missile, but this had no flames or smoke. The object was moving faster than a missile. As the object came close, everyone heard a roll of thunder in the distance toward the object. No one could tell that it was Martek. Martek came in fast and busted through a window on the third floor of the apartment complex. The firefighters outside heard the loud shockwave shortly after he flew passed.

"What the heck was that chief?"

"I don't know, but what ever it was, it's in the building."

Martek started to walk down the halls of the building shouting out for anyone.

"Is anyone in here? Say something!" He shouted out.

There was a lonely firefighter, who was sitting in the corner of a room on the second floor on the other side of the building. He coughed as the smoke thickens. With his last dying breaths, he shouted out for help.

"Help!"

Martek turned around and an echo was heard ringing into his ears.

Help!

He heard the word help, and looked into the direction where the sound came from. He remembered the mall and started to concentrate on the walls, making them transparent. When he looked toward the second floor, he saw someone sitting in the corner coughing. He ran as fast as he could to help the stranded firefighter. When he got to the apartment where the man was, he broke through the door and ran up to him.

"Come on, we have to get you out of here now!"

The man looked at him.

"Who are you?"

"There is no time for that; we have to get you out now."

Martek reached for the man and lifted him up over his shoulder.

"Hold on." Martek said to him.

The fire made its way to the main gas tank of the complex and exploded. Martek jumped out of the window next to him and flew away from the explosion that was caused by the gas. The entire complex exploded into flames and crumbled to the ground. Martek landed in the back of the complex at the parking lot and put the firefighter down onto his feet.

"I can't thank you enough kid. Who are you? Please let me know."

Martek looked and smiled at the firefighter.

Martek's face was completely covered in ash, concealing his identity.

Crowds of people, firefighters, and news reporters came from around the corner and frantically headed toward them. Martek looked over to the man he saved.

"Just a friend." He said as he turned around to run away.

He leapt up into the air, and with a roll of thunder disappeared into the sky. The fireman waved up.

"Thanks again."

Back at the newsroom, Martek's Mom was given a brand new sheet of paper, as news from around the world started to pour in about the caped hero.

Martek flew into his attic and headed to the living room, where he watched the television that he had left on. He saw his Mom on the screen.

"Good afternoon and thank you joining us today. This Special Report comes to your from right here in Riverdale, when just today an apartment complex was engulfed by flames. There were no deaths and minimal casualties. But that's not all there was. One of the reporters caught this video tape of a caped man actually flying into the air, leaving the scene of this event. If you look closely, the figure is wearing a blue cape of some sort and a dark costume. Of course after seeing someone like this in public, you couldn't help but to laugh. But this was no joke. The caped man actually flew up into the sky, leaving nothing but a loud boom of what sounded like thunder. Today the caped man is being dubbed the caped hero. Witnesses are saying that they saw him enter the building and save the very last person stuck in the burning complex. We interviewed the firefighter he saved and this is what was said."

The firefighter appeared on the screen.

"I don't know what it was that saved me, all I know is he is an amazing guy. If it wasn't for him, I wouldn't be coming home tonight to my family. Thank you, whoever you are." The fireman said.

"Did he say anything to you? What did he look like? Is he human?" The reporter asked.

"This guy is human. He told me that he is just a friend, and he looked just like you and I do. He is just a regular person with a very welcoming voice. I can't thank him enough and I wish I could shake his hand."

"Thank you. You and your men did a great job today. You are all heroes." The reporter said.

"Thank you."

The screen showed his Mom again.

"Well there you have it ladies and gentleman, it is definitely clear that there is a new superhero in town. If you have any details, please contact us as soon as possible. We'd love to hear from you. For now, authorities and the public are calling him Nighthawk. So if you can hear me Nighthawk, keep up the good work."

He shut off the television.

"Nighthawk? The name is Martek. Ugh, I hate that name!"

He walked to the bathroom and looked at himself.

"That's strange... My suit has nothing on it, but my face is covered in ash."

He washed his face and suddenly felt tired. He walked to his bed and got under his covers and fell fast asleep.

Hours later, his Mom woke him up. Martek was still in his costume, and he covered himself with his blankets more and more so she didn't see what he was wearing.

"Are you okay?" She asked.

"I'm fine. I just got tired, that's all."

"Are you sure?"

"I'm fine Mom. How was your day?"

"Today was really weird. Have you been

watching the news?"

"No."

"There was a fire downtown, and some guy dressed as a superhero came in and saved the day."

Martek laughed.

"A superhero; what was his power, bravery?"

"No, this guy is on every news station now. He has been nonstop ever since the news came in. He flies and supposedly he has supernatural powers. Some say he is an alien, others say he is human."

"Okay… I find this hard to believe." He said.

Martek knew that it was him, but in order to keep his Mom from finding out, he had to hold off for just a bit longer.

"Well if you want to see for yourself, go look at the television. I bet it's on the internet as well."

She walked out of the room and closed the door behind her. He got up and quickly got out of his costume and into his regular clothes. He took a seat at his computer desk, and turned on the computer. When he signed online, he checked his email. He saw an email from Ashley.

Hey Martek,

Wow, today was really interesting. What happened to you? All of my friends are talking about you. How did you change so much? I know you do wear long sleeved shirts an awful lot at school but this time after seeing you I just had to ask. You were many times over Rod's size and what's even more; you kicked Rod to the ground and beat the heck out of him. I hope you are okay. I saw Hampton chase you around the corner but I guess he didn't catch you. Just let me know how everything is, I am worried about you. Also, have you heard the news lately? If not, you should watch it. There

*is supposedly a real live superhero out there. Anyways,
that's beside the point. Email me back and let me know if
everything is alright.*

> *Always,*
> *Ashley Holt.*

When he was about to respond, Druid messaged
him.

MasterDruid: Dude, are you okay?

GreatMartek: Yeah, I am fine. Long day today.

MasterDruid: I bet, guess who I saw all over the
blasted news.

GreatMartek: Gee, I wonder who it could have
been.

MasterDruid: Yeah, well that was awesome. I
can't believe the abilities you have, how did it feel?

GreatMartek: It felt great. I just got really tired
or something. I'm not used to this kind of stuff.

MasterDruid: And I swear I am laughing so hard
at your name. Hi Nighthawk!

GreatMartek: Shut up Druid, I can't believe they
gave me that name.

MasterDruid: You should find a way to get this
changed.

GreatMartek: Don't worry; I have an idea I think.

Martek's Mom went to the phone and saw that there was one new message. She listened in on it.

"Hi Ms. Majestic, this is Deputy Hampton. Martek was involved in a fight today at school. Although he is not at fault, he is being suspended from school for a week. He ran from a police officer and we think he needs some time to think about what is going on. You need to talk to your son because we are concerned of his behavior..."

Sarah continued to listen to the message. Meanwhile, Martek was writing a letter back to Ashley.

Dear Ashley,

Thanks for the email, it was thoughtful. Today was a really weird day but don't worry I am fine. I just went home and so far no one has come to my house. I haven't heard much about the guy on the news, but I have heard enough about him to know what is going on. It seems like a lot has happened today. I hope you are doing good and I can't wait for your reply. I better get going. I'll talk with you later.

Yours,
Martek

Martek sent the email to Ashley. Just then Martek heard his Mom.

"Martek! Can I see you out here now?"

"Coming!"

Martek got up and walked down the hallway where he saw his Mom sitting at the dining room table.

"Martek, have a seat."

Martek sat down.

"Hun, the school called. They said you got into a fight and ran from the police?"

"I was scared Mom. I got into a fight but it wasn't my fault."

"Yeah I know it wasn't, they said that on the machine. Martek, what is going on? Is something troubling you at school? And why are you so different. You are wearing clothes that are layered, and I barely see you anymore. You have all those weird things going on in your room and I don't know if I even know who you are anymore."

"It's nothing Mom, I promise."

"Okay but if there is anything, please let me know."

"I will."

"By the way, you have been suspended from school for a week."

"What?"

"I'm not mad, but while you are suspended, I want you to keep this house clean, and I want you to think about what is going on with your life. You have changed."

"Okay."

Martek walked down the hall and into his room with a sad face.

"Have I really changed in a bad way? I want to tell her so much about me, but I can't." He said to himself.

He got back onto the computer.

GreatMartek: Okay, I am back.

MasterDruid: What's up?

GreatMartek: I'm suspended from school for a week.

MasterDruid: That's obvious!

GreatMartek: Yeah. Hey dude something happened to me today after school. There is this one guy in my dreams that looks extremely evil. He appeared in my dreams several times and at the park down from my house, he came to me. Dude he told me the story about this sword and everything. Supposedly it is the sword of some ancient God who was killed by the dude.

MasterDruid: Okay, what is this dude's name?

GreatMartek: The evil guy is Solaro, the sword belongs to a guy called Lunaro. Lunaro is the God of the Moon and Light, Solaro is the God of the Sun and Fire.

MasterDruid: That would explain the kind of abilities you have. Remember I said you have energy for your main power?

GreatMartek: Yeah, that must be it. But him and I got into an energy fight and let me tell you, I have never felt so energized in my life. I found a cool way to get my sword too. I am afraid of it though because I don't know how to hide this thing. If the sword is in Solaro's possession, he said that the whole universe will be his.

MasterDruid: Okay this is getting a little too weird.

GreatMartek: What do I do?

MasterDruid: I don't know. Just find a way to hide your sword a lot better. I have to get going though; I'll talk to you later. Bye man.

GreatMartek: Later Druid.

Later on, after dinner was done, he decided to fly around and see what there was around the city. He got into his costume and looked out of his room door. His Mom was sitting on the couch in the other room so he knew it was time to leave. He floated up into the attic and flew out of the broken glassed window heading straight into the sky. His Mom heard the faint thunderous sound from down the hall. She got up to see if Martek was okay.

"Martek?" She asked.

She walked toward the hall and saw the news having a story on the caped hero.

"Martek!"

She ran down the hall in excitement.

"Martek the news is on about that one guy I told you about!"

She opened his door and found out that he was missing.

"Martek? Where did he go now?" She said.

Circling the downtown buildings of Riverdale, he practiced his free flight. He enjoyed every minute of it, as it made him as free as a bird. Flying with the sword in his hand he looked around to see if anything could be done. He flew over the apartment that burnt down earlier today. He saw some of the clean up crew packing up, and getting ready to go home. Suddenly, he heard a loud thud below him echo in his ears. He looked down to see what it was but could only see a large building below him. He flew down to take a closer look, and spotted a large black delivery van at the back entrance of the building. He flew around to take an even closer look and saw four men wearing all black, and wearing masks. The men were hauling many bags into the van.

"What in the world?" Martek said.

He looked up and saw a sign on the building,

which read Riverdale City Bank.

He knew right then that these guys were robbing the bank. One by one the robbers finished what they had to do, and got into the van.

"Oh no you don't." Martek said as he flew down. The Van started up.

"Alright, that was too easy guys!" One of them said.

"Yeah, it's like taking candy from a baby."

They all laughed in excitement.

Suddenly they felt the van rise up.

"What the heck is going on?" One of them said.

"Hey man, what is it."

"I don't know, but I'm going to find out."

One of the robbers opened the sliding door on the side of the van and looked under the vehicle. Martek looked at the guy and smiled. "Hi." Martek said.

The guy got up quickly and told them what he saw.

"Guys, there is someone out there."

"Well what is he doing?"

"You won't believe this. But he is holding up the van."

"Holding up?"

"Yes, he has the van in his hands. I swear I am not lying."

"Alright, enough of this." One of the robbers said as he unbuckled his seat belt.

The robber leapt down from the side of the van and took out his gun from his jacket. He looked at Martek.

"Alright pal, I don't know who you think you are but you better put this van down now before I put a bullet in you."

"You mean this van?" Martek said.

"Look, I won't ask you again." The shooter said

as he pointed the gun at him.

Martek yawned.

The shooter fired a shot at Martek, but the bullet bounced right off of him.

"What the…?" The shooter said in disbelief – taking aim to fire again. He fired again and the bullet bounced off once more.

"Hey are you okay out there? What's going on?" One of them said in the van.

The shooter opened fire on Martek, but Martek had had enough of him. He took the van and tossed it at the shooter, killing the shooter instantly as he and the van smashed into a brick wall.

The robbers climbed out of the van in anger and rushed toward Martek. All of them started to fight with him. Martek fought back, fist after fist, he hit them into the walls behind them. They grabbed chains and guns, and started to give Martek all they had. It was no use.

"Why won't this guy die?" One of them shouted out.

Martek walked up to the two in front of him, and took them by the neck and threw them into the van behind them; which knocked them out unconscious. The third guy came behind Martek with a rope and jumped on his back. He put the rope around Martek's neck in hopes to choke him but it was no use. Martek reached behind him and grabbed the guy by his jacket, and tossed him into the bank window. The alarm set off as he smashed into the glass. Martek walked toward the van and then heard the echoing of sirens headed his way.

Out in the front of the bank, police vehicles flooded the area. They got out and ran in every part and angle of the bank. When they got to the back, they were shocked at what they saw. They saw the four robbers hanging upside down on a rope, about two stories up in front of the bank's back entrance.

"What the heck is this?" One of the officers said.

They looked below the robbers and saw stacks of bags in a pyramid shape leading to a point at the top. Everyone was stunned at the sight. One of the officers went to the dark side of the bank, which glowed bluish white in the alley way.

"Hey Chief, you got to take a look at this!" One of them said.

The chief and a few officers walked over to the officer and saw a glowing symbol that was carved into the concrete.

"What is it Chief?"

"I don't know."

The news crew started to pour in on the scene and came several feet of the spectacle on the concrete floor.

"Keep those people back!" The chief ordered his men.

Officers crowded the news crew and pushed them back from the scene. One of the cameras managed to get a shot of the symbol on the ground, and was soon blocked by an officer's hand. Unaware that the symbol was photographed, the police didn't bother to gather any evidence from the news crews.

Martek was flying higher and higher away from the bank as he saw the sirens below him flashing throughout the city.

"Wow that was neat! I can't believe what had just happened. I stopped four guys from getting away with what could have been the biggest robbery in this city."

Martek flew back to his house and into his attic window. When he got into his room he got out of his costume and put it away. He walked down the hall.

"Where have you been?" His Mom asked.

"I was out for a walk; I had to get some things off of my mind."

"Oh okay, well sit down; they are talking about

something that went on just now at the bank."

Martek took a seat across from his Mom and watched the television. He watched the news and saw the robbers being carried away by the police. One of the robbers did nothing but complain about what happened.

"I'm telling you guys, it's a huge monster!" The robber screamed out loud.

All of the robbers were left with bloody faces.

Martek sat there and smiled as he watched.

"Wow, isn't that something?" She asked.

"Yeah it is. Hey Mom, I am kind of tired, I'm going to bed."

"Alright, Goodnight Hun."

"Goodnight Mom."

Martek got up and headed to his room. He got into his night clothes and fell fast asleep.

CHAPTER 9

Martek woke up and got ready for the day. He made his own breakfast at supersonic speeds. Within seconds, everything was done. He did the house chores in seconds, which normally took hours. He turned on the television and there was still news coverage from last night. He saw a glimpse of the M that he had left on the ground, as a clue to tell everyone who he was.

"And last night, one of our cameramen was able to catch a shot of the symbol on the ground. Police were very secretive of this phenomena, but weren't successful in guarding this image. As you can see from this image, it is carved into the ground along with a distinct letter M. Some people are saying that it could be part of his name. All we know for sure is he wasn't seen at the bank when authorities arrived and there is no physical evidence that Nighthawk struck again. The only evidence is this letter that lasted for only several minutes. Currently, the area is blocked as we have reports of the letter actually still being there, carved into the cement itself."

"Way to go Mom." He said.

"Also, we have a special weather statement for you for tonight and tomorrow morning. Scattered showers will appear this evening, which will break out into heavy thunderstorms. Counties such as Riverside, Riverdale, and Martinsville are under a Severe Thunderstorm Watch. A tornado watch has also been issued for the same county areas. Stay turned for more live coverage after a word from our sponsors."

Martek turned off his television and thought of what he could do today. He got up and went to his room to get his sword, but it was missing. He looked all around for it but could not find it. He frantically began to worry.

"Oh no, Solaro must have taken it!"

He had an idea that might work to get the sword back. He thought about the time he and Solaro got into the fight out in the park. He raised his hand into the air and the sword appeared into his hand.

"Oh there we go. Where in the world did you go?"

He practiced his powers and his sword fighting skills some more. Hours later, he heard a knock on the door.

"Now who could that be at twelve in the afternoon?"

Martek ran to the door and looked through it. He saw John, Druid, and Eric standing there. He opened the door.

"Hey guys!"

"Hey Martek, it was minimum day at school today, so we decided to visit you." Druid said.

"Sure come in!" Martek said.

Eric looked at Martek in a short sleeve shirt, and stared at him, not believing his eyes.

"Dude Martek, what the heck happened to you? Are you on Steroids?"

Martek laughed.

"Just come in guys."

They all came in and sat down on the couch.

"Alright Eric, I feel you need to know this." Martek said.

"Okay…?" Eric listened in.

"Remember when I was lost in the forest?"

"Yeah."

"Well, something amazing happened to me up there and it has turned me into something more."

"Okay."

"Do you know that guy they have all over the news now?"

"Yeah, Nighthawk or whatever."

"No his name isn't Nighthawk."

"Okay, what is it?"

"His name is Martek."

"Wait a minute. What?"

"It's true. I am that superhero that is on the news. I wanted to tell you so much sooner, but I just got the hang of these abilities."

"Okay… And John and Druid knew about this?"

"They were there when I found the sword. They found me in the forest."

"Oh okay. Wait a minute… What sword? You didn't mention a…"

Martek raised his hand above him and the sword appeared behind blue energy surrounding him.

"Whoa!" They all said.

"Well at least you know how to get your sword if you ever forget it!" Druid laughed.

"Yeah I know huh. But Eric, you can't tell anyone yet about this. I trust you."

"I won't, you can always trust me. Man this is so

cool though. You can fly and everything?"

"I can do everything."

Druid faced Martek.

"Martek, you mentioned to me about the sword, but where has it been this whole time?"

"Solaro said something about the Realm of Power."

"The Realm of Power?"

"Yes."

"Do you know if this Realm exists anymore?" Druid asked curiously

"I don't know."

"Well because a thought occurred to me. Since that sword was protected in that place this entire time... Why don't you cast it in there and take it out when ever you want?"

"That's not a bad idea. I just don't know how to get it inside of the realm."

"Have you even tried?"

"No."

"Try it right now, I bet you can."

Martek concentrated hard onto the sword and raised it above him. A bright light engulfed the sword and it was gone.

"Of course, I remember when I couldn't find the sword, it was missing and then I got it by doing that same thing, only it appeared in my hand; not disappeared! I get it now! The sword was in the Realm of Power when it was missing but I retrieved it when I called for it."

"Sounds kind of like its own defense system!" John added.

"Well, we have to get going. It's been fun and we will talk with you later. Everyone said hi at school." Druid said as he got up.

"Okay Druid, tell them I say hey. Have a good day you guys. Eric thanks for listening."

"No problem Martek, thanks for trusting me."

They all walked out of the house and Martek shut the door behind them. Martek wrote a note to his Mom and put it on the refrigerator saying he'll be right back. He got into his suit and again he blasted out of the attic and into the sky.

With dusk approaching, he decided to fly to the ocean. He could feel the cooler ocean breeze as he got closer. At supersonic speeds, it took no time to get to the beach. He saw behind him the cities fade away, covered by the Riverdale Hills as he headed west. As he got closer to the beach, the clouds got thicker and thicker until he was covered in a thick layer of clouds. He felt water particles splash into his face. He flew down lower to get out of the cloud layer. He saw the beach approaching.

Down in the rough waters, a coast guard ship was fighting desperately to save a woman who was caught in the strong waves. The waves were deadly and starting to take over the woman completely. The coast guard rushed to save her but nothing was helping. Then, the woman sank under the stormy waves and was gone.

"Where'd she go? We lost her!" One of the men shouted out loud.

"No we need to keep looking!" Another one shouted.

Seconds later, they saw something coming in from onshore. Martek raced at super fast speeds and dove straight into the ocean making a large splash. They all looked and waited in anticipation, but still after a few seconds nothing. Then, they saw a burst of water explode up into the sky, followed by Martek; who was holding the woman in his arms. Martek glided down onto the deck of the ship.

"Make room men!" One of them said.

He landed and slowly, putting the woman down

on her back.

"Stand back, everyone. Give her room." Martek said.

The woman started to cough up water, and Martek helped her catch her breath.

"You're okay now. Its okay, you're safe. I got you." Martek said as he held her.

The woman looked up into her heroes eyes and smiled.

"Thank you. Who are you?"

Martek smiled.

"Just a friend."

Martek got up and turned to the coast guard.

"She's all yours guys." He said as he turned away.

He ran to the edge of the deck and took off like a speeding bullet, back east toward the city.

He got home, and just as he was getting ready to get out of his suit, he saw another special report on the news.

"I'm Sarah Majestic. Just minutes ago, another sighting of the caped hero was reported just off of the Riverdale Beach; where a young woman was saved from drowning in the furious stormy ocean. Live we have Tim on the scene, Tim can you tell us what's going on?"

"Thank you Sarah. Just moments ago this woman was saved by the hero himself. She said that he had welcomed eyes, and a soft face. He looked no older than her seventeen year old son, just a teenager. Reporting live from Riverdale Beach, back to you in the studio."

"Thanks Tim. Well there you have it. The hero has been identified as a possible teenager. More on this story and him, when we return."

Martek turned off the television and heard drops of rain start to hit the roof above him. The storm has arrived.

About an hour later, the rain began to pour so intense, that the roads were already flooded. He began to worry about his Mom.

"She should have been home by now. Where is she? Maybe it's just traffic."

He turned the television on to see what was going on, and a special report came up on the news.

"A silver sedan is stuck under the Santa Ana River Bridge, when just moments ago, this car lost control and slid off of the street and down onto this hill. We have reports of a woman in this vehicle; emergency and fire crews are trying their best to reach her. Our biggest concern right now is that the car is slowly going under the bridge. If this car goes any further, it will be smashed and the driver will be killed."

Martek took a good look at the vehicle and recognized it right away. He figured it out, and without any time to waste, he blasted out of the front door and headed to the bridge faster than he has ever flown before.

He got to the bridge and saw helicopters and emergency vehicles all around. He saw the news stations filming the event. Martek flew down there, and the news crews saw him and started video taping everything.

Martek's Mom was stuck in the car, struggling to get out. The water was now up to her chest slowly taking her over. The windows and doors were jammed, and she couldn't get out. She screamed violently for help.

"Someone please help me!"

Martek landed on top of the car, and she heard him yell out.

"Get down!" He yelled.

She got out of the way on time; as Martek punched through the roof of the car, pealing it away to get to her. Martek ripped the entire top of the car off, and tosses it into the river. She looked up at him and both of them saw eye to eye.

"Martek?"

"No time to explain, Mom. I have to get you out of here. Take my hand."

Martek grabbed her hand and lifted her up into his arms, and flew away from the car up into the sky and out of sight. The car was then engulfed by the raging waters of the river. Martek's Mom looked up at Martek, and around her as they were flying back to the house. She fainted on the spot. Martek looked down and smiled as they flew back home.

At the house, Martek walked to the living room and laid his Mom on the living room couch. She woke up and looked at him.

"Mom?" Martek asked.

"Martek?" She asked back.

"Yes, it is me."

"Martek, why didn't you tell me?"

"Because, I didn't want anyone to know."

"Is this why you have been so different?"

"Yeah."

She looked at him in the costume and couldn't believe it. She saw the emblem and the sword and how much muscle he gained.

"Martek, what happened to you?"

"I found this sword when I was lost in the Riverdale Hills, and it's given me special abilities. I have sworn myself to use these for good and to help others."

"Did you make your costume?"

"Yes, I did."

"Renaissance project, huh?" She smiled.

"I'm sorry Mom; I was going to tell you."

"Thanks for saving me Hun. I Love you so much, and you are the best son no matter what."

Martek smiled.

"Thanks, please don't tell anyone. I know you work for the news and this would be the biggest story of your career, but please don't say anything."

"I won't. I am glad it is you and not someone else. I still don't know how and why."

"Me either Mom."

"Okay well, I am going to get dinner ready."

"I'll set the table!"

Martek moved at super speeds and within seconds the table was set.

"Okay Martek, don't show off now." She smiled and laughed.

"I'm going to get changed."

"That's a good idea."

Martek raced down the hall and got out of his costume and sat down to go online. He checked his mail and got nothing. Then, Ashley messaged him.

RiverdaleChk: Hey Martek.

GreatMartek: Who is this?

RiverdaleChk: It's Ashley.

GreatMartek: Oh hey Ashley, good to hear from you.

RiverdaleChk: Same here, how is everything with you?

GreatMartek: Things here are good so far... Nothing bad going on. Just enjoying my suspension.

RiverdaleChk: Yeah I heard you were suspended. I'm sorry.

GreatMartek: It's okay.

RiverdaleChk: Hey do you know anything about that mysterious guy on the news? Like do you know him?

GreatMartek: Kind of.

RiverdaleChk: Really?

GreatMartek: Yeah, I kind of do.

RiverdaleChk: Wow that is neat! Hey I have a question. One of my friends asked me something I am kind of curious about it. She wanted to know if you liked me.

A long pause came over Martek. He was stunned and couldn't find the words to say.

RiverdaleChk: I mean, I was just curious.
GreatMartek: What would make your friends say that?
RiverdaleChk: I don't know, I guess I was just wondering cause...
GreatMartek: Cause what?
RiverdaleChk: Cause I kind of like you too.

A long pause came over Martek. Everything seemed so pure for him. He had long waited for her to say that one little thing, and there it was, in all its digital glory.

She sat there wondering what was going on. Embarrassed that she said it too soon, she quickly signed off before Martek could reply.

"No!" Martek said out loud.

He panicked and then remembered where she lived. He always saw her go home in middle school, so he knew where she was. It was the house across from the middle school with the large tree out front.

"Dinner!" Martek's Mom yelled out.

Martek ran down the hall and ate his dinner. During dinner, the news turned on and there was a storm warning and a potential tornado warning in the western area of Riverdale.

"Wow, this is quite a storm." Martek said.

"Yes it is. I had an interview with the Ontario Weather Service and Kevin and Josh were calling this a big one. It looks as if they were right again. The other stations called for heavy rain and periods of thunder. I don't call these periods, I hear thunder every second; so far and it looks like a lightshow outside."

They both laugh.

Then a loud crash of thunder was heard causing the power to the house to go out. About five seconds later, the power switched back on.

"Wow that was a close one!" She said.

They looked at the news.

"Alright this is official; a tornado has been reported moving down western Riverdale headed for the Northern section of the city."

"Northern?" Martek asked.

"That's what he said."

"That's us."

Martek looked at his Mom and she knew what was on his mind. She nodded her head and smiled. Martek ran down the hall and got into his costume. He raised his hand above him and the sword appeared before him. He ran down the hall and stopped in front of his Mom, who was sitting at the table.

"How do I look?"

"Like my Son."

Martek smiled and bolted out the front door to beat Mother Nature. She ran to the door and watched him fade away into the lightning filled sky.

"There goes my Son." She smiled.

Martek raced for the area where the report came from. Just ahead of him, he saw the tornado. The tornado was huge, almost a half a mile wide. He knew that this was going to kill lots of people as soon as it got into the neighborhood area. He quickly thought of ways to get rid of it. Suddenly, he had an idea. He raced to the tornado, and flew around it in the opposite direction that it was spinning. The force started to throw the tornadoes rotation off track, and the tornado faded into nothing but a low hanging cloud.

Martek on the other hand, was completely faded out from the motion that he fainted and fell to the field below him. The storm around him started to subside and only faint rumbles of thunder could be heard. The rain had stopped and the storm as nearly over. Martek was now lying in the field unconscious.

Martek jumped out of his unconsciousness and looked around to see that he had landed in a field. The storm was over, now seen in the distance away from the city. He got up and flew into the sky back home. When he got into his room, he fell onto his bed fast asleep.

CHAPTER 10

Martek woke up and looked outside and saw that the sky was crisp blue with only a few puffy clouds left in the sky. The sun was shinning, and the ground was glistening with water left over from the rain, which was turning into steam by the warm sun.

He got out of bed and got ready like he normally did. His Mom was at work, so again he had the whole house to himself. After he finished getting ready for the day, he turned on the television, and then he had an idea.

"Wow, I have been using the remote this entire time. I was so used to it I completely forgot about everything else."

He took the remote and turned off the television. After careful thought, he concentrated on turning it back on, but this time with his mind. After a few seconds, the screen flickered and the television turned on. He practiced flipping the channels and this seemed to have worked nicely.

"Wow! I could get used to this!"

He went into the kitchen and started to make his breakfast. At supersonic speeds, something made him stop what he was doing. He rushed to the television and watched the news. They were having a report on the storm that had hit last night.

"Last night, severe thunderstorms broke out all over the forecasted area. Surprisingly, no one was injured. There was one car that was lost at the now broken Santa Ana River. Alternate routes are to be made if commuting over the river bridge. There were several reports of a tornado by many citizens of Riverdale; however that isn't the only thing that witnessed this wild weather event. As you can see here, Doppler radar indicated a severe thunderstorm with a distinct hook shape to it. The hook is actually the spin in the thunderstorm itself. The hook was so pronounced that it had produced a large tornado. Analysis shows that this tornado was nearly a half a mile wide with winds in excess of two hundred miles an hour plus. In the next frame you can see that the hook was completely destroyed. In the animation you will also see the storm died out in just seconds. Weather experts call this an impossible action for any storm and it goes against the laws of anything ever known. We are not sure if our caped hero has anything to do with this, but if he has, we thank you again."

Martek finished making his breakfast, and sat down to eat it. After he finished his breakfast, he quickly cleaned up the house and the kitchen and thought about what he could do today. He thought about getting into his costume and just seeing if anyone needed any help, but he had no reason to as today, was more of a clean up day from last night's storm. Then, he thought of something. He remembered when Ashley had confessed to him that she liked him. He remembered that she signed off in a hurry. She must have felt bad or something. He had an idea and he hoped it would work. Before he would do anything, he would just fly around the city to see if anything needed to be done. After school got out he would meet up with her. He got into his costume and blasted off into the sky.

Martek flew around the city, but everything seemed extremely quiet. Some areas that were hit by the tornado were already being cleaned up. Today looked like a decent one.

Hours later, Ashley got off of the bus and was walking home. She got into her house and slowly walked upstairs.

"Hey Ashley, are you okay?" Her Mom asked.

Ashley stopped and turned around.

"Yeah Mom, I guess I am okay. I just had a really rough night last night online."

"Care to tell me about it?"

Ashley sat down on the step and her Mom walked up to sit beside her.

"Well, it's about this guy I like at school. I have always noticed him and thought he was great, but never got to really say anything. Then last night, I told him that I liked him, and he didn't answer me back. I felt so embarrassed I just decided to sign offline and go to bed."

"Well dear, maybe he was shocked and likes you too? Maybe he was just what we like to say, at loss for words. I mean in a speechless way."

"You think so?"

"Sweetie, you are beautiful, of course he notices you. And you have a great personality and everything."

"Thanks Mom."

She hugged her Mom.

"By the way, do I know this guy?"

"Yeah…"

"Who is it?"

"Mom!"

"I'm just curious."

"His name is Martek."

"Oh that boy, he is such a nice guy, I like him. Shy, but nice."

"Yeah he is. Well Mom I'm going to go upstairs to my room."

"Okay dear, dinner will be ready in a couple of hours."

"Thanks Mom."

Ashley got up and walked to her room and closed the door.

"Teenagers." Ashley's Mom said shaking her head smiling.

Ashley put her stuff down and jumped on her bed face down putting a pillow over the top of her head. Then she heard a knock on the front door.

Ashley's Mom walked to the door and opened it.

"Hello there, Mrs. Holt." Martek said.

"Why Hello Martek, my you have grown since I last saw you."

Martek smiled.

"Thank you. Um, is Ashley home right now?"

"Yes of course she is, let me get her. Hold on just one second."

"Okay great. Thank you."

Ashley's Mom walked up to her room and knocked on the door.

"Ashley?"

"Yeah Mom."

"Someone's at the door for you."

"For me? Who is it?"

"It's Martek."

"What! Okay... I'll be right out!"

Ashley panicked in a good way but nonetheless she ran around her room like a chicken with her head cut off.

"Oh my God, what do I do? Is this okay to wear? How is my hair?" She said to herself as she ran around.

She rushed to her dresser and looked in her mirror.

"It's not that bad. Oh wow, okay… I better get going."

Martek was standing out in the entry way at the front door talking to her Mom. Ashley walked down the stairs and her Mom walked into the kitchen.

"Hello." Martek said.

"Hi…" She said crossing her arms blushing.

"Look, can we talk?"

"Sure."

"Alone?"

"Okay…"

"It's rather important."

"Okay… Let me go tell my Mom. We'll go walk around the neighborhood."

"Okay, no problem."

Ashley went to her Mom in the kitchen.

"Hey Mom, Martek and I are going out for a walk around the block. We will be back in a bit."

"Okay, be back before your Dad gets home. You know how much he hates waiting to eat dinner after a long day of work."

"Oh mom, how can Dad have a long day at work? He's always out in the backyard in the garage; probably doing his ridiculous experiments." She smiled.

"Yes I know, but your Dad is a brilliant man. Have fun and I'll see you soon."

"Thanks!"

Ashley walked down the hall and took her jacket from the coat rack. She walked past Martek, and opened the door.

"Let's go." She said as she held the door open.

Martek walked outside and she closed the door

behind her. They walked across the street along side the school's chain link fence.

"Hey Ashley, do you mind if we talk over in the football field right there."

"No, not at all, we'll have to hop the fence first."

"Hop?" Martek asked, forgetting what the word even meant.

"Yeah, you know, get over it and climb to the top and jump down?"

"Oh okay…" Martek smiled.

They both got over the fence and walked over to the middle of the field. The sun had just set and the twilight was amazingly blue out. It was a rather cool evening because of the storm that went through. The grass had dried up from the warm sun earlier that day. They went and sat down on the grass. Both of them just looked at each other in the eyes. Ashley smiled.

"Martek, you are making me blush."

"I'm sorry, I can't help it."

"Why didn't you answer me last night?"

"I was shocked, I totally like you too Ashley. I have always had a crush on you, ever since the day I laid these eyes on you. I think you are amazing and I was happy to hear that you like me too."

"Really?"

"Yes Ashley, really."

"Wow."

"Look I want to be honest with you and I like you a whole lot." Martek said.

"I like you a whole lot too."

They both stood up and held hands facing each other. With her looking him in the eyes, they mesmerized themselves and got lost in their own senses. Suddenly, she looked down to the ground and grabbed a hold of Martek, holding him tight.

"It's okay, I got you."

She looked around him and back into his eyes.

"Wait a minute… You're… that guy everyone is talking about. You're the guy who's been on the news. How can this be?"

"It's a long story." He said.

"You're… what is your name? You never told anyone yet."

He looked up into the sky and smiled.

"I'm Martek. Now hold on!"

He raised his hand up and off they went, straight up into the sky. Ashley looked below her and saw the field get smaller and smaller. He took her hand and they flew above the city. With the city lights below and the twilight sky above, this was indeed a wonderful sight.

"Oh wow! I never thought I'd see anything like this! It's so beautiful!"

"Yeah, it is wonderful, but not as wonderful and as beautiful as you."

The near full moon could be seen over the horizon ahead.

They both looked at each other deep in the eyes.

"Look out." Martek said smiling.

Ashley looked ahead; she saw a thick white cotton ball about to hit them. She closed her eyes tightly and they went right through the cloud, feeling the water particles splash into their face.

They both looked at each others wet faces and laughed.

Minutes later, they land on the very top of the Riverdale Peak to the North of the city, and look down at the city. They sat holding each other talking.

"So does this mean you might not be going to school often?"

"Well no, school will still be there. It just means that I may skip some time in case anything happens."

"Can you tell me how this happened to you?"

"Well at my birthday party everyone went and played some laser tag up in the Riverdale Hills, it was fun. Then I was running in the forest, when all the sudden I tripped. I tripped and fell into a ravine and woke up. I looked around and couldn't really figure out where I was. I saw the moon above me, and the sky was just like how it is now. I walked through the forest and I saw a circle of trees. A light appeared from up into the sky, and a sword appeared in the middle of the circle of these rocks. I took the sword, and then John and Druid found me some time later, and we went home. After that, I noticed that I was getting weird abilities, and it all added up to here. I found out my true meaning when I stopped some guy from robbing a store last Sunday."

"Oh wow, that is really hard to believe. But then again, everything so far has been amazing. No one knew who stopped that guy at the mall, but I do now."

"I wanted to be honest with you Ashley. I just want you to know that you mean so much to me. My new purpose for these powers is to guard the sword from getting into my enemies hands."

"You have enemies already?"

"Well to make a long story short. My enemy wants my sword because he has one just like it. If he gets my sword, he will be able to take over the entire universe."

"Who is this enemy?"

"His name is Solaro. He claims he is the God of the Sun and Fire."

"Have you seen him?"

"Once, we got into a battle just minutes after I flew away from Deputy Hampton."

"It was you that did that loud crash of thunder."

"Guilty." He smiled.

"And your sword... Where does it come from?"

"It is a sword of another God. His name is

Lunaro. Solaro said he was God of the Moon, Light, and Energy."

"What happened to him?"

"He was killed in a battle with Solaro. Before Solaro could get the sword he wanted, Lunaro cast it into a secret realm called the Realm of Power. Lunaro said when someone comes along who is true at heart; they will be given the sword, which will turn them into what Lunaro was."

"Lunaro didn't have a cape and called himself a Superhero though."

"I know. This is what I chose on my own to do. I also will protect the sword. I have it in the Realm of Power right now. Only I can take it from that spot."

"That is a lot to take care of. I don't want you to get hurt, but I knew you were different somehow." She smiled.

They both smiled back at each other and looked back at the city lights.

"Come on Ashley, I better get you home. I don't want you to be late for your parents."

She took his hand and they both flew off back to her house.

They landed in the field across the street from her and said their goodbyes. She hopped the fence and walked to her front door. Martek waved at her, and raised his hand up into the sky. She saw the sword appear in his hand, and transform him into his costume. She smiled and waved back. Martek took off into the sky rather slowly. She watched him fly higher and higher until he was gone.

Martek was flying around in content, and extremely happy. He had done what he wanted to do for the longest time. The girl he always liked finally said she liked him too. He felt lighter than air, even though he was able to fly. The stars were coming out and the sun was long gone. The near full moon was shinning brightly on him in the crisp and clear sky. Then all the sudden, he had an idea.

"I wonder where this all started.   I should find out now."

He raced for the Riverdale hills. When he got there, he flew on top of the laser tag area. He spotted the two rock formations right away, and then he found it. The circle of trees was very small to the west of the formations in the middle somewhere. Just then, a bright yellow energy ball shot up so fast, he couldn't dodge it. He was struck with so much force; he lost all senses and fell straight to the ground.

After a while, Martek started to regain his consciousness. He slowly started to get up. He looked at his hands and then himself.

"Wait a minute… I remember this from somewhere." He said as he had a case of Déjà vu.

He slowly got to his feet and looked around. A dark shadow suddenly covered him. He looked behind him and saw the silhouette of a dark and mysterious figure in front of the moon, whose eyes glowed bright yellow.

"What do you want?" Martek shouted out in anger.

"You know what I want. Give me the sword."

"I don't have it."

"You're lying!"

Solaro rose up his staff and gathered so much energy, a bolt of lightning shot straight at Martek hitting him to the ground.

"Now give me the sword."

Martek got up and brushed himself off.

"Alright. You want to play that game?" He said.

Martek too the sword out of the scabbard and stood in fighting stance.

"Then let's play!" Martek said shooting a beam of energy at Solaro.

Solaro blocked the energy with his staff and used it against Martek, by absorbing it into his staff. When all of the energy was absorbed, he shot another bolt of lightning at him. Martek blocked the first bolt with his sword and tried to slow time down enough to dodge the second, but the bolt was too quick. Unable to beat the speed of light; it knocked him onto the ground again, making him roll until he was face down.

"Well, well, well... Martek is human after all." Solaro said walking up to him.

Martek slowly got up and got to his knees in utter pain.

"Now I am going to ask you one last time foolish boy. Give me the sword now!"

Martek took the sword in his hand and gripped it with so much strength. He slowly stood up and faced him.

"Never!" Martek said out loud.

"This was your last chance."

Solaro gathered the energy again and shot a lightning bolt straight at Martek. Martek took the sword and forced the lightning bolt to absorb into it. He gathered the energy from the bolt and swung the sword into Solaro's direction releasing the lightning bolt. The bolt hit Solaro, and he fell to the ground. Martek ran up to Solaro and swung his sword down at him. Solaro raised his staff with both hands, and blocked the hit. Solaro got up and kicked Martek back into the trees behind him, knocking over one tree. Martek got back up and ran up to Solaro, punching him in the face. Solaro flew back and hit a rock behind him. They both started to fight each other, both not able to dodge many punches. Since they both had powers, their use for speed was no use. Martek's sword and Solaro's staff were at a cross block.

"If you're so powerful, then why am I still alive?" Martek said laughing.

"Don't worry, your time is coming!"

"Likewise!" Martek screamed.

They pushed each other away. Martek raised his left hand and gripped a ball of energy into it. He shot it at Solaro and hit him to the ground. Solaro was so angry he returned fire multiple times. Martek dodged most of the balls, but was hit by a powerful one that sent him flying into the air. Solaro got up and ran toward Martek. Martek angry now, got up and ran up to Solaro and started to punch him left to right. One by one he landed each punch, and Solaro was growing weak. When Solaro was on the floor being punched left and right, he took the staff and smacked Martek to the ground. Solaro got up and pointed his finger at Martek.

"You haven't seen the last of me, Martek!"

Solaro raised his staff and struck it into the ground, causing a cloud of energy to engulf him until he was gone.

Martek got up slowly and looked around with a heavy breath. He walked over to the circle of stones where he found the sword. The stones were regular stones and nothing more. He looked around, and then up at the moon. He got to his knees.

"What am I!? What do you want from me?"

He looks down to the ground in sadness and tears

"Martek..." A voice from above said to him.

He looked up to the sky at the moon.

"Lunaro?"

"Martek, you were chosen out of millions for the purest of all hearts. You will guide my sword and legacy. I was once like you, but Solaro defeated me. Before he could get his hands on the sword, I banished it into the Realm of Power where it was protected against him to keep it safe, until the truest of all men would be able to retrieve it. Now you have it, guard it well as you shall join me after your life; passing on your legacy to the truest of all persons after you."

"If Solaro gets the sword, what will happen?"

"If he gets his hands on the last of two power swords, he will use it to control the universe and destroy this world and everything in it. This sword must never fall into the wrong hands, it is made to protect and not destroy. This is why you were given such abilities. I leave you now Martek, for my time on Earth grows short. I now go to the Realm of Spirits, my final resting spot. Please take good care of the sword, you are the one now. Guard it wisely. You are the one; you are the keeper of this sword, my avenger… You are Martek."

Lunaro's voice fades away.

Martek looked up and smiled.

"I will Lunaro… This I promise, I will."

Suddenly, a cloud of light appeared around Martek's sword and belt buckle. In bright blue white coloring, Martek's symbol 'M' appeared on the sword's hilt and the buckle. Martek looked down and smiled. When the light faded away, a carved M was seen on both the sword and the buckle. Martek looked up at the moon and smiled.

"Thanks Lunaro… Thanks."

He flew off away from the spot and back to his house.

When he got home he went to his room and checked his mail. He got an email from Ashley.

Martek,

I don't know what to call tonight, but I had a great time. You are way awesome and I really think you are just the best thing in the world to happen to me. You make me really happy and I can't wait until you do get back to school so I can see you again. Stay safe and don't worry... Your secret is safe with me.

> *Love Always,*
> *Ashley*

Martek smiled and his Mom yelled from down the hall.

"Martek, is that you?"

He got up and walked out to his Mom.

"Hey Mom, it is me."

"Where have you been?"

"I was visiting Ashley."

"Oh okay. Well the school called and they reduced your suspension time to only three days. You can go back to school on Friday."

"Oh that's cool."

"Just remember... No crime fighting until you get your homework done. I don't want any excuses."

"I won't Mom, I promise."

"Oh and can you run to the store and buy some matches? The fireplace won't light."

"No problem, Mom."

Martek pointed his finger to the fire place and shot tiny balls of hot energy into the fireplace and lit the fire.

"There you go, Mom."

"Very funny, Martek."

Martek smiled and walked to his room. He emailed Ashley back.

> *Ashley,*

> *Thanks for the email and thanks for everything! You make me happy too and I am glad you didn't freak*

*out on who I was and I'm glad to hear stuff that you like
me. Hey I am going to be coming back to school on
Friday so that's a good thing! I'll see you then and I miss
you! Goodnight!*

Always Martek.

He got out of his costume and cast the sword into
the Realm and went to sleep.

CHAPTER 11

On a perfect Friday morning, Martek woke up and got out of bed. Excited that he was going back to school today, he got into the bathroom to shower. He opened the shower door and it broke right off the hinges.

"Whoops!"

"Are you okay in there?" His mom asked.

"Yes Mom, I am fine."

He laughed and got into the shower.

Later on, Druid was waiting at the bus stop. Druid sees Martek.

"Hey Martek, what are you doing back so early?"

"Hey man, they let me off early!"

"That's great to hear. Wow you look great. You're not afraid of the short sleeve shirt look?"

"Who's going to do what about it?"

"Yeah that's true."

The bus came and they all got on.

Later on, they all got off of the bus and inside of the gates. With Martek wearing his short sleeves, it was no wonder why the whole school was looking at him. Martek was indeed the biggest guy in school, now three times bigger than Rod. The bell rang, and Martek went to P.E.

In the locker room, he took of his shirt and got ready for the class. Everyone stared at him, but no one looked at him or got in his way. When Martek locked up his locker and headed for class, everyone made way for him as he walked to the blacktop where his class number was. Mrs. Wells did role call and told the class today's event.

"Today is going to be the final tennis challenge. There will be four people to a team; each team will play to the win. The last team to win gets a prize at the end."

One of the students raised their hands.

"What's the prize Mrs. Wells?"

"Lunch with me at a restaurant of your choice."

The class got excited.

"Alright class, go to the courts and let the games begin!"

The class frantically ran to the courts.

"Except you, Martek." Mrs. Wells said.

Martek was stopped in his tracks by Mrs. Wells.

"How have you been lately? And how come you have changed so much?" She asked.

"I just had a good week, that's all."

Martek smiled and ran to join the rest of his class.

During the game, it was Martek's turn to serve the ball.

"Service!" He yelled.

Martek hit the ball to one of the players.

"I got it!" She yelled out.

The ball came fast and she swung at it and hit thin air. She looked and saw that the ball had burned a hole into her racquet. Then, everyone looked at the gate behind her and saw a hole in it. They looked back at

Martek in shock.

"Sorry guys…" Martek said smiling.

One of the guys got the ball and started the game on his serve.

"Okay Martek, this time lets not hit the ball too hard."

They got a good game going and the ball was being hit back and forth, for what seemed like minutes. When the ball finally came in Martek's direction, he swung at it and the ball flew up and over the court until it was out of sight.

"Oh come on! Where did it go this time? And what did you do while you were gone?" One of the players said.

"I'm so sorry guys. Look, I will just watch, I don't have to play."

Martek sat on the side of the tennis court and watched.

Meanwhile, the tennis ball flew straight out of the Earth and into orbit.

At lunch that day, Martek and his group were talking about his change and how he beat Rod up to a pulp that one day. Then suddenly, Principal Kosh got onto the speaker.

"Attention students. Today after school is our annual Strongest Man at School Contest."

"What? I didn't know the contest was today!" Martek said.

"Better sign up Martek, you'll win for sure." John said.

"No it's okay guys; I'll pass on that one."

They listened in on the announcement.

"Sign ups are being held all lunch at the quad, please bring school ID. Also, tickets are being sold there for two dollars each. The contest consists of weight training; such as bench pressing, curls, dead lifts, and more. Also, events featuring the shock put, one on one wrestling, and so much more. The event is three hours long, and snacks and beverages will be available at the snack stand at the corner west end of the football field. All students are encouraged to sign up or attend this event. One of the contestants who will be competing is three year champion senior football quarterback Rodney Burns! Don't miss this event!"

The transmission faded and was gone.

They all turned to Martek and started screaming.

"Come on Martek, you have to do it!" John said.

"Yeah Martek if you don't we are going to keep bugging you until you do." Druid assured him.

"Come on!" One of the others said.

"Yeah do it." Eric said.

Martek backed away and couldn't take this anymore.

"Alright everyone shut up!"

They were all silent.

"Alright, I'll go sign up. I'll do it."

The group cheered.

Martek and Druid walked to the sign ups, and Martek took the pen and signed up. Druid took the pen after and signed up as well.

"There, we're in."

Martek and Druid walked back to the group, and finished off lunch.

At the event, the bleachers were filled with students and the crowd was excited. This was a nice sunny and clear day, and the crowd was wild. Everyone was getting settled into their seats with just minutes to go until the contest started.

Martek was in the locker room getting ready for the contest. He put on the tank top that was given to him by the officials for the events. The tank top was black with a white number ten on the back of it. In the front, a white letter R was visible. Rod got ready and passed by Martek, both looking at each other. Rod nodded his head angrily and ran out of the locker room. Martek shortly followed after.

Principal Kosh was on the loud speaker making the announcement.

"Thank you, and welcome to the Riverdale's High School Strongest Man Contest!"

The crowd cheered loudly.

"Introducing today's contestants. Representing the sophomores are Jason Jones, Burt Williams, and Tommy Helt! Representing the juniors are Timothy McNeil, Bob Pratt, Druid Roberts, and Martek Majestic!"

Everyone started to cheer.

"Go Martek!" Ashley and her friends cheered on.

"And now, put your hands together folks for your Riverdale High School Seniors class of 2001! Travis O'Neil, Russell Hopkins, and your three time champion Rodney Burns!"

The crowd went wild and got to their feet as the contestants ran out into the field. Banners with their names were held up by the crowd, mostly for Rod and Martek.

"Let the games begin! Up first we have the dead lift. Players, approach the weights."

They walked up to their weights and stood there waiting for the command. The coaches put the weights together and waited for the first contestant.

"Each contestant will start off with two hundred pounds and an increase of twenty-five pounds after every successful lift is made. The Student, who lifts the most weight properly, wins. Up first is Timothy McNeil, a junior five foot seven weighing in at one hundred seventy-five pounds."

Timothy approached the weight and waited for the go. When the go was given he lifted up the weight with little of a problem. The weight was then added twenty-five more pounds.

"Okay, Timothy has completed two hundred pounds and will now attempt two hundred twenty-five pounds."

Timothy lifted the weight only half way up and failed to complete the rest.

"Oh… Too bad for Timothy; he only got to two hundred pounds, nice try Timothy."

The crowd cheered.

Time flew by, and all the contestants completed their tasks.

"Okay folks, we have so far Druid Roberts in First Place at three hundred pounds, Travis O'Neil in second place at two hundred seventy-five pounds, Russell Hopkins, Bob Pratt, and Burt Williams tie third place, and fourth place goes to Tommy Helt. Jason Jones was disqualified from the round. Up next is Senior Rodney Burns! Rodney Burns, who is six feet one inches tall and weighing in at two hundred thirty pounds, will attempt to take first place."

Rod attempted three hundred pounds and made it without a problem. He made every single weight after that and stopped at four hundred pounds.

"And Rod takes first place at an astonishing four hundred pounds leading by one hundred pounds, putting Druid in second."

The crowd cheered Rod on.

Rod walked next to Martek.

"Beat that one buddy." Rod said.

Martek smiles.

"Up next is Martek Majestic who is six feet two inches tall and weighing in at three hundred fifteen pounds."

The crowd gasped in amazement.

"What!" Rod yelled out.

"Wait a minute folks… Okay official statement here folks this is outrageous. Martek himself has just told us that he will begin where Rod left off. He is attempting to make the tie on his first try. Can he do it?"

Martek reached to the weight and looked at it. He then was given the go to lift and so he did. He lifted the weight struggling a bit so he could conceal his true strength.

"He's almost there folks."

He lifted the weight to the final lift and held it there for the allotted time.

"Martek claims the tie!"

The crowd went wild. Rod put both of his hands in his face and stomped onto the ground.

Martek raised his hand up as a signal to add more weight.

"What is this? I haven't seen this before folks but it looks like we have Rodney Burns a match. Martek is not going to take the tie; he is going straight for the win. He will now attempt four hundred and twenty five pounds."

Martek was given the go and he lifted up and got a little over half way up. He started to shake as the weight was too much for him. He knew that this was very light but he needed to make sure no one could find out his true strength. He looked at Ashley in the crowd and she smiled. He smiled back and lifted the weight straight up into the air.

"And Martek takes first place!"

The crowd went wild as Rod stomped the ground in anger.

"No, that's not fair! How could this be?" Rod screamed in anger.

"Ok folks. For this round we have Martek Majestic in First Place, Rodney Burns in Second Place, and Druid Roberts takes third. Up next we have the

Dumbbell Curl. In this round, each contestant must lift one dumbbell and do one complete curl. The curl will start from fifty pounds and increase five pounds after that. Up first, we have Burt Williams."

Burt Williams made the fifty pound curl, but failed on the sixty pound attempt. Timothy McNeil tried the fifty pounds but failed the first try, which disqualified him from the round.

As time passed by, Druid and Travis were in first place, at seventy five pounds. Second place went to Bob Pratt and Russell Hopkins at seventy pounds. Third place went to Jason Jones at sixty five pounds.

"Up next is Martek Majestic!"

The crowd stood up and cheered Martek on with everything they ever had. Some banners that read Rod on them had been switched to Martek, which made Rod mad. Martek knew that he needed to lose some rounds to keep this a fair game. Martek curled up until ninety five pounds and stopped.

"Martek takes first at ninety five pounds!"

The crowd cheered him on.

"Up next is Rodney Burns."

Rod gave the signal to go higher then where Martek had left off. He gave the signal for one hundred pounds and curled it with ease, dropping the weight and walked away to take the winning point.

"Rodney Burns takes First place by five pounds as he curls an astonishing one hundred pound dumbbell. This will put Martek Majestic in second, and Druid Roberts and Travis O'Neil in third."

The crowd gasped as they couldn't believe Martek was beat. They were certain that Martek would wipe the floor off of Rod in that round, but they were surprised. Ashley knew that Martek was keeping this game fair, so she watched with a smile and with no worries.

Over an hour later, it was time for the last and

final round. The score was Druid with two, and Martek and Rod with four. Everyone else was out of the contest

"Alright folks, we have a final round. Druid Roberts is officially third place of this contest. Congratulations Druid!"

The crowd cheered as Druid walked toward the bleachers and high fived his students above.

"But now, the final round... Arm Wrestling!"

The crowd cheered. Sudden 'yeses' and 'yeas' came from the crowd.

"It all comes down to two students; Rodney Burns and Martek Majestic. The student who wins this event will be dubbed the Strongest Man in the School, and given three hundred dollars cash!"

The crowd roared in excitement as banners of Rod and Martek were being held high.

Martek had let the contest go this long, for this very event. He knew that this would indeed be what he had been waiting for.

"Will the contestants please approach the table?"

Martek and Rod came face to face staring at one another at the table. The coach came up.

"Alright you guys, take your seats. We are going to keep this good and clean. If I see anything wrong in this event you will be disqualified from the round."

Martek and Rod took their seats and cupped hands. The coach positioned their elbows and wrists in the proper direction and held them tight. The coach blew his whistle letting go of both hands. The crowd went wild as Martek and Rod battled it out. Both of them looked at their grips, still not one of them was moving to either side. The hold lasted for many minutes.

"This is Pathetic." Martek says to himself.

Martek knew this was indeed pathetic, he wasn't even trying yet. Rod on the other hand was already breaking a sweat. Martek pretended a bit harder by making himself sweat and his face a bit redder. After two minutes, Martek slammed Rod's fist straight onto the tabl,e breaking the table in half as Rod was thrown down to the ground off of his chair.

"And Martek wins the contest!"

The crowd cheered as they rushed onto the field to congratulate him.

"Martek Majestic is now the Strongest Man in the school, which breaks Rodney Burns' winning streak!"

Martek was taken over by the crowd and hand shakes and pats on his back were given. Ashley ran through the crowd and jumped on Martek, giving him a big hug. Martek hugged her back and the principal made his way through the crowd. He walked up to Martek and handed him the three hundred dollar check and a large trophy in his name; which said Riverdale High School's Strongest Man of 2001. They shook hands and got their picture taken. John and Druid ran up to Martek.

"You did it man! Congrats!" John screamed.

"I knew you could!" Druid said.

Martek held up the trophy with one hand and everyone else touched it to help with the celebration.

CHAPTER 12

Martek got home and decided to play a game on his computer. Meanwhile, Rod was at home in his room lying on his bed looking up to his ceiling; listening to the radio talking quietly to his self.

"No good Martek. The contest should have been mine. How in the hell did this happen?"

He laid there listening to the radio, when all of the sudden it started to static. The static turned to complete and utter noise, which was the same sound when your television has no reception. Rod got up to fix it, and right when he was about to touch it, something happened.

"Rod…"

Rod heard the voice come from the radio and fell straight back and hit the floor. He slowly got up and walked toward the radio.

"No… That can't be." He said.

He looked at the radio again.

"Rod… Go back to the High School field at seven." The voice said.

The voice faded away and the radio tuned back to his regular station.

"What in the…"

Rod looked at his clock, which read six. The school was down the street from him, so he ran out of the house as soon as he could.

Martek was in his room talking to his friends online and reading a few emails; he picked up the phone and called Ashley.

"Hello?'

"Hi Ashley, its Martek."

"Hey you!"

"Hey, Listen, John and Druid are going with me to the mall at seven tonight. Would you and a few of your friends like to go with?"

"I'd love to! I have Erica and Jessica over here right now. You are on speaker phone and they are shaking their heads yes."

Martek laughed.

"Okay great, then we will see you out front at seven then."

"I can't wait, bye Martek."

"See you soon Ashley."

They hung up the phone and got ready to go.

Martek told John and Druid online that they were going to be going to the mall and a few girls were coming along. Druid and John were very happy and got ready right away. John was with Druid at his house right now and they were going to be getting a ride from Druid's big sister Christina.

Martek got ready and just as he was about to rush out of the door, he was stopped by his Mom.

"Congrats on today Hun, I bought you a present."

She handed him a large white box.

Martek opened it and was amazed.

"Oh mom, this is perfect! Thank you so much!"

He got two pairs of large pants and XX-Large white t-shirts. He ran down the hall, and then ran back to his mom to get changed in less than 3 seconds.

"Wow that was fast."

"Thanks Mom! I'm off to the mall with my friends. I will be back in a few hours."

"Have fun. Do you want me to drive…? Never mind." She laughed.

He smiled and walked out of the front door to the side of the house. He looked around him, but no one was looking. He took a giant leap into the sky and shot up like a shinning blue bullet.

Martek's Mom was looking outside the front door, and heard the rumble of thunder in the sky; smiling as she looked to the sky.

"Be careful my Son." She said closing the door.

Druid and John were already at the mall waiting for Martek. Martek walked around the corner and met up with all of them.

"Hey guys!" Martek said.

"Hey man, glad you could make it."

"Thanks. Are the girls here yet?" Martek asked.

"Not yet, we are still waiting." John said.

"Oh okay, no problem, I am sure it's traffic. The freeway was pretty packed on the way over here."

"You mean looking down on the freeway as you gracefully flew past all of the traffic?" Druid smiled.

"Yeah… Something like that."

They all laughed.

"Hey Martek, I wonder how Rod's taking his loss." Druid said.

"I don't know, and I honestly don't care."

Meanwhile Rod entered the gate of the school just minutes before seven. He walked to the middle of the football field where earlier was packed by the entire school. He saw no one around, nothing but silence and darkness. He looked down at his watch.

"Almost seven."

He looked around.

"Man I must be stupid. A radio told me to come here. How lame can you get? I must be really losing it today."

Just as it turned seven, a whirl of yellow energy swirled in the middle of the field about twenty feet from Rod. The bright cyclonic energy thickened until a dark figure emerged from the light. The light faded away and the dark figure stood and stared. The sun had just set directly behind the dark figure. Rod stood there frightened.

"Hello? Can I help you?" Rod asked.

"I am Solaro, God of the Sun and Fire."

"Okay... What do you want from me? Was it you in my radio who spoke to me?"

"I am... I saw your defeat at the competition today, a pity. It must have been hard. Rodney Burns, three times in a row on this, and you were beat by a once small and pathetic boy."

"Yeah, well it's not everyday that you get beat by a small skinny twig, who all of the sudden turns into some freak of nature you know."

"Ah yes, Martek is it?"

"Yeah."

"Have you been watching the news lately?"

"Yeah."

"Then you know about the hero that just, came about. Do you not?"

"I hear about him all of the time."

"Doesn't it strike you odd that this hero and Martek have come in at just about the same exact time?"

"Wait a minute... You're not saying."

"Saying what!"

"Nothing... I just... That Martek and this

mysterious hero is the same person?"

"Bingo. You are smarter than you think."

"Of course, that means Martek cheated today."

"Quit with the contest already, you failed to win and that is final. But wouldn't you like revenge Rod?"

"Pay back? You bet I would."

"Good, then I need your help."

"What do you want me to do?"

Just then, a bright light of energy appeared in the distance to Rod's left. The energy faded as a glowing sword appeared, floating and spinning above the grassy field. The sword was identical to Martek's, however it had a more of a golden hilt, not a silver one like Martek had. A golden letter M was seen on the top of the hilt shinning in its own inner glow.

Rod turned back to Solaro.

"What is it?" He asked.

"This sword is one of two. Martek has one, I have this one. I keep this in a safe place until I am certain I can get my hands on the other sword. I trust you to do me this favor. Take my sword, Rod. By taking it you will have powers beyond your wildest dreams."

"I see an M on the sword, what does it mean?"

"It was named after the man who created the two swords; a man of great power, who is long gone now."

"I see, and what is it that you want me to do?"

Solaro Smiled.

"Destroy Martek."

"Destroy Martek? I can't kill him."

"Why not? He plans on taking over your reputation; he's taken so much from you. It's time to take something from him."

"It's murder."

"Do you want to be the most powerful being on Earth?"

"Well, I guess."

"Then kill Martek, and bring his sword to me."

Rod was in heavy thought as he looked back to the sword. He slowly made his way to it. The sword spun with power and energy all around it. Solaro stood in the distance watching him. Rod looked at the sword and reached out to grab the hilt. With a burst of energy, he was surrounded by bright light, as the sword stuck into his hands and gave him what Solaro had promised.

At the mall, Martek, John, and Druid were still waiting for the girls to arrive. Martek got a strong ringing in his ear and closed his eyes tight.

"Hey man. Are you okay?" Druid asked.

Martek snapped out of his mood.

"I think so. It was just an ear tone, that's all."

Just then Ashley, Erica, and Jessica came around the corner.

"Hey guys!" Ashley called out.

Martek ran up to Ashley and gave her a hug.

"Hey Ashley."

"Sorry we are late; Erica took forever with her make-up."

They all laughed.

"That's okay." Druid said smiling at Erica.

Erica smiled back blushing.

"So should we go inside?" Martek asked.

Everyone agreed to go inside and they entered the mall entrance.

Rod's teammates Travis and Russell were also at the mall. Being that it was Friday night, many people from their school went to the mall. Martek was given shout outs and pats on his back from earlier today. Everyone smiled.

"Wow dude, you really are quite the celebrity." John said to Martek.

They made their way through the crowd and past Travis and Russell, which were walking the opposite way they were walking. When Travis and Russell walked by the restrooms, they were both grabbed and pulled into the hallway.

"Where is he?" Rod asked them both.

"Where is who?" Travis asked.

"Martek. Where is he?"

Rod began to crunch both of their shirt collars.

"Take it easy man, we saw him pass by over there about one minute ago." Travis said.

Rod looked at both of them with glowing yellow eyes, and shoved them both back into the wall behind them, and walked toward the direction Travis pointed.

"What the heck was his problem?" Russell asked Travis.

At the food court, Martek and the group were sitting down at one of the tables. They were chatting and having a good time snacking. Suddenly, a loud sound like explosion occurred; which threw people and other objects all around. Martek looked around and got up. He walked to the side of Ashley and looked back. He saw a small snack stand flying right for her. He rushed and grabbed her, as they both fell onto the ground and rolled into one of the tables. The snack stand missed all of them and smashed through Ashley's seat, and into the store on the other side of the aisle. Everyone in the mall was now at a panic, running to the nearest exit.

Martek got up and looked around. He helped Ashley up to her feet.

"Are you okay?"

"I'm fine. What is going on?"

"I don't know."

Both of them ran up to the rest of their group to see if everyone was alright.

"Is everyone alright?" Martek asked.

John and Druid had the girls held tight.

"Everything is fine. Martek, you shouldn't be

over here right now." Druid winked.

"I know, look, go to the emergency exit right there to the side of the mall and make your way to the front. This is no place for you guys and you know it."

"But, Martek, what about you?" Ashley said.

"Don't worry. Now go!"

Martek gave Ashley a hug, and then she was grabbed by the rest of the group. They all ran to the exit to leave the building as things were crashing all around.

Martek ran to the restroom and went inside. Seconds later, he came out in full costume; sword and all. When he got to where he was sitting, he saw a large dark figure standing in the middle of the food court, who was staring at him. The figure was wearing a black armored suit, with a black hood and yellow piercing eyes.

"Solaro, don't do this! Many people are going to die!"

The voice gurgled with anger.

"Who are you calling Solaro?" I am Corod, Apprentice of Solaro. You Martek are finished!"

Corod raised his right hand into the air. All around, yellow and white lightning bolts started to strike his closed fist. Energy from all around him started to stir up as a bright central light thickened around his fist. Suddenly, a sword appeared in Corod's hand.

Martek gasped, and took one step back.

"It is the other sword." Martek said softly to himself.

Martek stared up at the sword, which was emitting yellow energy from the blade.

Without hesitation, Corod rushed to Martek at extreme speeds to slice him. Martek quickly blocked the blade with his blade. Both of them fought with their swords in a cross blade position.

"I will kill you once and for all." Corod said.

Both of them were still in a cross blade position as

they pushed with all their might. Corod was indeed strong, as Martek couldn't push him away. Corod kicked Martek in the chest, and he flew back hitting the wall behind him. The wall crumbled with pieces of marble and concrete.

"Pathetic Martek, I'll crush you with my bare hands."

Martek got up slowly and stood straight up. He realizes he must use all of his skills in order to stay alive. Martek walked over toward Corod, not determined to strike back. Corod clenched his fists and raised his left hand. His eyes began to glow bright yellow, as a ball of energy appeared in his hand. Corod threw the energy ball toward Martek, but Martek used his laser vision to blast it away. He did so a few more times, which made Corod angrier.

"Okay, now it's my turn." Martek said.

Martek took his sword and powered it up with blue energy. He blasted the energy out of his blade, knocking Corod to the floor. Corod quickly got up and took a product stand from the side of the aisle, and tossed it at Martek. The product stands shattered into millions of pieces, as it hit Martek's glowing body. Martek had used his body as a shield against the flying object.

Just then, the mall doors busted open. A swarm of Police officers flooded the entrance.

"Alright both of you drop your weapons! Now!" One of them said.

Corod looked over at Martek, and Martek looked at Corod. Corod started to walk toward Martek as officers opened fire, but Corod was too strong for the bullets. Sparks were seen bouncing off of his body. He punched Martek in his face and grabbed him by his belt. Martek was thrown at the officers with so much force; it blew them all out of the building and into the parking lot where everyone was outside watching. Many officers were seen flying out of the mall; smacking into the asphalt, trees, and vehicles.

Ashley saw Martek roll onto the ground.

"Martek!" She yelled.

She started to run toward him, but was stopped by John and Druid.

The building started to catch fire from the inside, and it was making its way around the front entrance. Seconds later, Corod emerged from the flames and headed outside. Corod raised his hand and absorbed some of the flames, blasting them toward the police units. The flames hit the units and explosion after explosion occurred. Martek started to get up. Corod grabbed a light post, and pulled it out of the ground. He walked toward Martek, as he got up. When Martek stood straight up, Corod swung the light post at him and flung Martek back into a row of cars. The row of cars smashed into one another, and caused a wave of cars to fly back onto the main highway. The cars on the main highway slammed on their brakes, trying to dodge the scrap metal on the road. Soon, a pile up occurred on the road, and many were injured.

Martek regained his strength, and got up. Corod tossed the light pole to the side, and started to walk toward Martek angrily. Martek got up and flew into his direction at high speeds. Before he got to Corod, he extended his foot out in front of him making a flying kick move. He kicked Corod with so much strength, that he flew back into the marble wall of the mall, and was gone. Martek stood there breathing heavily. The whole crowd watched in anticipation.

Suddenly, dust kicked up from all around and made a cyclonic dust storm with energy and light, surrounding the inside of the mall.

"This isn't over yet, Martek!" A voice echoed into the air.

The dust and energy flew off into the air and was gone. Everyone around was now talking about what happened. They all started to help people. Emergency vehicles flooded the scene, and the main highway.

Martek looked around for his friends and Ashley. He saw them and ran up to them.

"There you are guys. Hey I have to go, but I'll talk with you guys later."

Ashley's friends stood there shocked.

"Martek?" Jessica asks.

"No time to explain ladies."

The Police start running toward Martek.

"Got to go!"

Before the police could catch him, he flew off at supersonic speeds into the air.

Ashley's friends had questions, but John and Druid made them promise not to tell anyone.

Corod left the area leaving great devastation. The sounds of sirens and cries were heard echoing throughout the mall.

Corod stood on top of the tallest building in the city looking down at the mall. He saw helicopters and flashes of emergency vehicles all around.

"I was so close. Martek is stronger than I thought, but not next time. Next time he won't be so lucky."

Solaro appeared behind Corod. Corod turned to face him.

"Corod, you have failed me!"

"It won't happen again, just give me one more chance; he won't get away with it next time."

"Very well, I will give you one more chance to prove yourself worthy."

"I'll get you your sword, do not worry about that. Leave Martek to me though. He has made a fool out of me one too many times."

"See that the job is done!" Solaro vanished into

the darkness.

Martek flew into his attic, and jumped down to the hallway. His Mom walked up to him.

"I heard what happened. Are you okay?"

Martek was startled and heavily thinking.

"I'm okay Mom, I just need some time to think, that's all."

Martek walked into his room with a blank look on his face. He got onto the phone, and called Ashley on her cell.

"Hello?"

"Ashley, it's me."

"Martek!"

"How are you? How is everyone?"

"I am fine, everyone is okay too. We are just a little shaken up, that's all. Right now we are waiting for the parents to come and pick us up. Are you home already?"

"Yes, I just got home. Did any of you guys get questioned by the police?"

"No, they were too busy getting everyone to safety. We are at the side of the mall right now where all of the police are escorting people to safety."

"Okay, that is good, as long as you and everyone else are okay."

"Yeah we are fine. Who was that guy?"

"I don't know, but I'm going to find out."

But Martek knew who this guy was, and what he was after. He saw the sword Corod had, and how it looked much like his own. He knew Solaro was connected to this somehow, and was using Corod to retrieve the sword.

"Martek, our parents are here. I have to go. I will call you later."

"Okay, I will talk with you later."

"Bye Martek."

"Bye Ashley. Take care of yourself."

Both of them got off of the phone.

At Rod's house, he was in his room throwing darts at a picture of Martek, which he hung on the wall. He walked over to his dresser and took out his sleepwear to change out of his suit. When he got dressed he walked over to his mirror on the door and looked at himself.

"Whoa. I guess Martek isn't the only big guy around here anymore."

Rod was surprised to see that he was now as big as Martek. He walked over to his closet and took out a metal baseball bat, and bent it. After bending it, he snapped it and it broke in half.

"This is impossible." He said smiling.

From how he was at the mall, he knew he was super strong. Rod however, didn't realize that he would undergo the same change as Martek. He put on a muscle shirt and it ripped in half.

"This can't be happening." He said.

He slipped into a large sweater and walked out of his room. He went to the back door and opened it to go outside. He walked to the side of his house and climbed it until he got to the top of the roof.

"If Martek can fly, then I can too."

Rod took a couple of steps back as he faced toward the front of his house. He ran as fast as he could, and jumped up into the air. With a huge smile on his face, he thought he figured out how to fly. He jumped rather high, giving him the feeling of flight, but then fell to the ground smacking into the bushes in his front yard by the sidewalk.

Rod's Mom opened the front door.

"Hello? Is anyone out here?" She said.

She closed the front door; Rod laid face down on the other side of the bush. He lifted his face up from the ground.

"Maybe I just need to practice more. I really thought I could fly."

He got up and decided to go to the high school football field down the street. He walked into the field and got into the very middle of it. It was pitch-black and no one was in sight. He summoned his sword and it appeared before him. He was then transformed into his Corod suit.

"So my main power is my strength. Martek is strong too. How can I get around this?"

He stood there thinking.

"Martek may be strong, but I wonder if his heart is invincible."

A big grin crossed his face, as his eyes glowed bright yellow. Energy from all around surrounded him, engulfing his body as he vanished into thin air.

The following night, Ashley was sitting in her room in front of her mirror, combing her hair. She was about to go to bed for school in the morning tomorrow, when a bright light appeared behind her, revealing a dark shadow. She turned around and screamed.

Corod raised his hand toward Ashley, and she began to float into his grip.

"Silence!" He yelled out.

He took his hand and covered her mouth from screaming.

Ashley's parents heard her from downstairs and they both ran up the stairs.

"Ashley!" Her Dad yelled.

Corod looked over to her bedroom door and raised his hand toward it, shutting it on her parents before they could get in. Her parents tried to open the door, but it was jammed shut. The father tried to break it down, but it was no use.

Corod turned to Ashley and looked at her deep in

the eyes. She looked at his glowing yellow eyes in fright.

The father continued to ram the door, but it was no use. They heard Ashley scream. Energy from all around surrounded them both, and they disappeared into the darkness. The door finally loosened up, and her Dad broke down the door. They both rushed in to see where she was, but she was no where in sight.

"She's gone, call the police." Her Mom said.

Martek was resting on his bed when he opened his eyes. He heard the echoing of Ashley screaming into the air. He looked around and the scream faded away. He got up and into his costume, and flew out of his house at super speeds to Ashley's house.

When he saw Ashley's house below, he knew something wasn't right. He flew down to take a closer look. A police car was out front, and he flew to the roof of the house and landed gently. He used his X-ray vision to look through the roof of the house and into her room, where the police and the parents were talking about what happened. He listened in on the officers taking the report.

"Okay ma'am. You heard your daughter screaming?"

"Yes, my husband and I both heard it."

"Okay, and you and your husband ran upstairs and the door shut by it self as if someone slammed it shut?"

"Yes and my husband tried to break down the door, because it was jammed shut when we tried to open it back up. And then when he opened the door, Ashley was gone. It's like she just disappeared. The window was locked and everything."

"Okay ma'am, we will be on the lookout and check more into this. In the meantime, have you got into any contact with any of her friends to see where she might possibly be?"

"No, we heard our daughter scream and we

decided to call you guys first." Her Dad said.

Martek stopped from listening in and walked to the back of the house and stood there thinking.

"I wonder why she screamed. Where could she be?"

He thought hard on where she might have gone. He then had a feeling that Corod and Solaro had something to do with this. He wondered where they might have taken her to. He took off into the sky, and began his search into the night.

Druid was in his room blasting away people in his Counter-Struck game when he heard a tapping on his window.

"What the heck was that?" He said getting up.

Being that he lived in a two story home, someone had to have been on his roof. He went to the closet and grabbed a golf club. Another knock was heard.

"Who's there?" He said approaching the window.

"Hey Druid, it's me Martek. Open up man!"

"Martek?"

Druid opened the blinds and sure enough, it was his friend Martek floating about outside of his window in full costume.

"Open up man."

Druid opened the window.

Martek was floating there cross armed with a bewildered look on his face.

"Hey man, are you okay?"

"Dude, something happened to Ashley. Someone took her."

"What do you mean? Like a Kidnap."

"Yes, someone kidnapped her out of her room and the police were at her house. I've been searching all night with no luck. Whoever this was, they are very strong in their power because they are blocking my vision senses."

"Vision senses?"

"Yeah, my ability to see things with my mind. Somehow it is being blocked."

"Wow. Do you think it could be Solaro?"

"I am betting on it. The Police said that there were no traces of breaking and entering. They said it seemed like she strangely disappeared."

"Yeah, sounds like him to me. What about that guy at the mall?"

"Oh wow. I didn't realize that. I forgot about him. That's true it could be him as well!"

"Yeah man. Are you going to school later on today?"

"Today?"

"Yeah. It is Monday."

"No it is Sunday."

"No Martek, its Monday Morning. It's just about one in the morning right now."

"It's that late?"

"Yes, how long have you been searching?"

"I've been searching for hours. But dude I have to find her. And yes, I am going to have to go to school tomorrow. I'm going to skip though and I'll meet up with you at lunch somewhere. I'll find you tomorrow. Right now, I'm going to continue looking."

"Okay, be careful. Good luck man."

"Thanks."

Martek turned around and shot into the sky leaving nothing but a thunderous sound. Druid looked up and shook his head.

"Lucky dog."

CHAPTER 13

The very next day at school, Druid was waiting around for Martek in the volleyball courts on the P.E. blacktop. He knew that Martek would meet up with him there so he waited. A few minutes later, he felt a tap on his shoulder. He turned around to see Martek without his costume.

"Hey Martek."

"Hey man. No luck and I searched everywhere. I don't get it. It's really like she disappeared."

"Have you heard from Solaro or that other guy?"

"No, and that's the strange thing too. It's almost as if they are waiting for the perfect time to attack. I just have this feeling that is what they are planning to do."

"Man that is crazy."

"Tell me about it. So how is everything going today?"

"Well, rumor has it that Rod is pissed about the fight. He is so mad that he swears up and down if he sees you today he is going to fight you again."

"Are you serious? Wow, I am laughing. Really I am. I say bring it."

"I know that's what I am saying."

Just then a voice was heard from the quad toward Martek and Druid's direction.

"Hey there he is!"

Martek and Druid looked over and saw a crowd coming toward them. The crowd started to cave in on them. Martek knew what was about to happen. He saw Rod pushing his way through the crowds.

"Hey Druid, you better stand back."

Druid walked back and took front row in the crowd. Soon the entire school was there ready to watch Rod and Martek.

Rod walked up to Martek and got into his face.

"You took something from me last week. I know your game, and I know everything about you buddy. To me, you will always be a shrimp. As for you cheating last week at the games, I decided to take something of my own."

"Oh yeah? And what is that?"

"Your precious little Girlfriend."

A long pause came over Martek. His eyes began to widen.

"It was you?"

"That's right Martek, and I have a present for you."

Before Martek could answer, Rod took his fist and punched him in the face. Martek flew back and hit the ground rolling into the pole of a basketball hoop. The hoop broke and smashed to the floor.

Druid started to run toward Martek, but the crowd grabbed him back.

"Let them fight man!"

Druid struggled to get free but the crowd held him

tight.

Martek started to get up.

"You think you are something. Well you're not!"

Rod kicked him in the stomach, and Martek flew into the side of the gym. The gym was made of a very hard concrete substance, but Martek's impact made that part of the building crumble like sugar cubes.

Martek quickly got up as Rod was running to him. He grabbed Rod's neck and slammed him to the ground. Rod kicked him back. They began to fight vigorously taking hits to the face. Then Martek and Rod were joined by the wrist holding each other back.

"What happened to you? How did you get this strong?"

"You are pathetic Martek. Just as pathetic as you were in the mall this past weekend."

Martek lost his strength as he knew who he was fighting with.

"You... You're Corod."

"You might say that."

"Listen to me Rod, this isn't like you. I know Solaro has some kind of hold against you. Fight it, don't go with it. Tell me where Ashley is now! Where is she?"

"I'm going to end this once and for all. Oh, and by the way; go to the circle of trees tonight. My Master would like a chat with you."

Rod took Martek and lifted him up over his shoulders and threw him straight into the gym building. The force was so great that it knocked Martek unconscious on the basketball court inside.

Rod looked at the crowd in anger, and ran out to the end of the school yard and hopped the fence. He disappeared into the river bed below. Everyone heard the sound of someone very evil laughing, as the sound echoed into the skies above.

Everyone including Druid ran into the gym to see

if Martek was okay. Martek had disappeared too.

Later on that night, Martek flew over the Riverdale Hills. He cautiously looked around, to prevent last times incident. It was a crisp night, now with a full moon that hung in the sky above. He saw the circle of trees, and flew down to take a closer look. Inside of the circle of trees, he saw a bright yellowish globe floating in the center. He saw someone inside, and noticed right away that it was Ashley. He flew to it and got up to her face.

"Ashley!" He yelled out.

Ashley floated completely motionless as if she was stuck in time. Her eyes were closed shut, making her look lifeless.

Martek tried everything to get her out, but it was no use. The energy ball was so strong, that it was unbreakable. He knew that what ever had a hold on this ball, it was strong.

Suddenly, someone appeared behind Martek. He turned around and looked to see Corod standing there.

"Let her go, Rod! It's me that you want, not her!"

"It isn't you that I want, it is your sword. Give me the sword, and her life and yours will be spared."

"No! If you want it, you'll have to take it from my cold dead hand. And if you want to hurt her, you'll have to get past me!"

"With pleasure, Martek."

Corod fired a lightning bolt at Martek. Martek leaped into the air and rolled onto the ground. He took out his sword and blocked the second lightning bolt, reflecting it back to hit Corod. Corod was now upset as he rushed toward Martek. Martek got up and blocked Corod from hitting him. They battled it out in a large sword battle. Martek and Corod blocked every attempt to make a hit on each other. They found each other in a cross block again. Energy from each of the swords emitted from the center of the blades as they pressed onto one another.

"You're sword fighting skills are exceptional, Martek."

"Likewise."

They pushed each other away and started swinging the blades, causing sparks to fly as the blades clashed into each other.

"Tell me, Martek. Is this sword really worth losing your life?"

"It is. This sword isn't what I am keeping from you. If this gets into Solaro's hands, he'll destroy this planet and everyone in it. He will destroy all of mankind. The human race will no longer exist!"

Martek took Corod and hit him to the ground. Martek was just about to make his final kill, when suddenly he stopped. Corod took off his hood.

"What do you mean kill us all? He promised me power and that's what I want." Corod said.

Martek was surprised at the conversation being started, so he put his sword away slowly. He took Rod by his hand and lifted him to his feet. Then, without time to waste, Rod took his sword and jabbed it into Martek's upper leg. Martek fell to the ground on his knees in utter pain. Rod got to his feet and stood there gripping his sword with both of his hands. He raised it to the side and got ready to slice Martek's neck. Martek looked up in extreme pain, as blood gushed from his leg where Rod had stabbed him. Martek knew that the power in the sword was his weakness, as it made him vulnerable.

Solaro appeared behind Rod to watch Martek's death.

"Tell me again, Martek. Was this sword worth losing your life?"

"Rod, if you kill me; you'll die too. Solaro will destroy this planet and everything in it. Do you want to be responsible of that? Have you forgotten everything? Your Mom, friends, for God sakes visit your Dad for once. All of them, including us, will be destroyed."

Rod slowly brought down his sword and looked down in confusion and sadness. He turned toward Solaro.

"Rod, what are you waiting for? Kill him now!" Solaro screamed.

"Is this true? You were going to kill everyone, weren't you? You don't care about this planet. You are not the God of our Sun; you are the God of many other Suns. Answer me!"

"Look Rod, this isn't what it seems. That sword is stolen. I was only retrieving it, so I could return it to its rightful place."

"Don't listen to him Rod, it's a trick." Martek said.

Rod looked down at the ground not knowing what to do.

"Look Rod, I know we haven't been the best of friends, but you are still number one to me. You are better than Solaro. If anything ever meant anything to you, you would trust me with your sword. We can beat this guy, and save this planet and many others. What do you say?" Martek pleaded.

Rod looked up and nodded his head. He turned to Martek.

"You know what, I think you're right."

Solaro grew frustrated.

"No! I gave you an order. I created you, and I can destroy you too."

Rod reached for Martek's hand and lifted him to his feet.

"You know, I did enjoy having all of these powers… but I guess that isn't what makes me happy." Rod smiled.

Rod handed Martek the other sword. Just then, Rod's powers faded away, and he was in his ordinary clothes, being his old self once again.

Martek pulled the other sword from his scabbard and held both swords in his hands. Energy from all around surrounded him. Both yellow and blue energy engulfed him until the brightest white light ever seen came from within himself. The wound on his leg completely healed up, and his eyes glowed fierce bright white. The two swords were combined, to make Martek the most powerful being in the universe.

"No! I trusted you!" Solaro said pointing at Rod.

Solaro walked to Rod and swung his fist in his face, making Rod fly into a tree trunk, knocking him out onto the ground. Solaro turned to Martek and shot ball after ball of energy at Martek, but he stood there like nothing could touch him. The energy absorbed into Martek's body, and nothing more. Solaro tried harder to break the force field around Martek, but it was no use. Martek was too strong. He walked toward Solaro. Solaro swung at him, and Martek grabbed him by the neck and raised him off the ground. Solaro could do nothing but hang there and struggle. Martek threw him onto the ground. Ashley started to wake up, and she opened her eyes.

"Martek!" She yelled out.

Martek turned his head toward her. Solaro realizing that Martek was distracted, he reached for one of the swords and pulled it from Martek's scabbard. Martek turned quickly to see Solaro standing there with his sword in his hand. Martek loses the second power of the sword and went back to his other self. His eyes fade from white to regular.

"Alright Solaro, now we end this!"

Their sword blades met with sparks of energy flying in all directions. Solaro kicked Martek back and threw a powerful energy ball at him. He blocked the energy ball with his sword's blade, gathering energy into his blade. When the sword had enough energy, He pointed it at Solaro and shot a beam of light straight into his eyes. Solaro dropped his sword and covered both of his eyes.

"My eyes!" He screamed.

Martek quickly grabbed the sword from the ground. Solaro uncovered his eyes and saw Martek standing there with the two power swords in his hands. Solaro took one step back.

"No! This can't be!" He screamed out loud.

"Now, it's your turn Solaro!"

Martek took the two swords and thrust the blades into Solaro's chest, striking his heart. Solaro screamed in agony as the blades ripped through his flesh. The power swords he wanted so much were now penetrated into him. Martek pulled his sword out, but left Solaro's inside of him. Martek took a step back as Solaro grabbed a hold of his sword; gushing blood out of his mouth and chest. Solaro was now in extreme pain, as he started choking on his blood, he fell to his knees. Faint beams of light started to shoot out of him one by one. Energy started to take over his body as he started to vanish into nothing.

"No!" He screamed loudly.

Solaro exploded into tiny fragments of dust and light, which soon after left nothing but the sword behind. The sword fell to the ground and vanished into thin air.

He looked back and saw Ashley lying down on the ground. He put his sword away and ran up to her.

"Ashley, are you okay?" Say something!"

He held her tight, hoping that she would say something.

She began to open her eyes, and then looked over into Martek's and smiled.

Rod woke up and started to get up. He stood up,

feeling his head, which he felt like he was hit by a large truck. He looked over at Martek and Ashley.

"I thought I lost you." Martek said.

"You'll never lose me."

He gave her a big hug and a kiss on the cheek.

Rod interrupted.

"Alright you two love birds." Rod said as he walked over to them and touched Martek on the shoulder.

"No hard feelings, right Martek?"

Martek smiled.

"Yeah, no hard feelings."

Martek shook Rod's hand, and they all walked away toward home.

"So Rod...." Martek said.

"Yeah...?"

"How are you going to pay for what you did at the mall?"

"Oh... I'll think of something..."

They all laughed.

Throughout the world, the news had a final statement from the caped hero. News stations were relaying back his message.

"Although we may never know why these events unfolded here in this peaceful city; we do know someone is out there to protect and to serve. Recently, we have received a letter from our hero... Dear people of Riverdale and people of the world. For the past week, we have suffered many tragic loses, but have gained so much more..."

As the news broadcast was going on, Martek stood on the tallest building in Riverdale, overlooking the city in front of the full moon.

"...I will continue to protect and to help those in need as much as I can. Although I am still growing up into this world, I may not be there for all of you. But just know that I will do my best to lend a helping hand. I am your hero… I am a protector… I am Martek."

www.ingramcontent.com/pod-product-compliance
Lightning Source LLC
Chambersburg PA
CBHW030411020726
47493CB00003B/1031